WAITING
FOR GORDO

WAITING
FOR GORDO

by Sue Knight

First Published 2017 by Fantastic Books Publishing

Cover design by Gabi

ISBN (eBook): 978-1-912053-67-4
ISBN (paperback): 978-1-912053-66-7

This book is dedicated to Colin and to the Aramco Shoal with whom I spent many happy small island holidays – none of which, thankfully, turned out as this one does. With thanks also to the Giant Cockroach who came to my rescue by flying out of a suitcase at just the right moment.

SMALL ISLAND

THERE WERE TEN GREEN BOTTLES HANGING ON THE WALL, TEN GREEN BOTTLES HANGING ON THE WALL, AND IF ONE GREEN BOTTLE SHOULD ACCIDENTALLY FALL ... Miranda swayed dizzily, she was so high up, the wall was so narrow, the crash of breaking glass so frightening ... She could not keep her balance forever and when there were no bottles left then she too would topple slowly and inevitably into the void. One by one they fell and smashed somewhere far out of sight ...

The noise grew louder as the drinks trolley advanced down the aisle, and Miranda's head fell forward so she woke again, cramped and uncomfortable. At last it was daylight. Immense fields of cloud were holding the plane in the sky above the endless fall, reminding her of something she had been dreaming of – something important that had fled away with the stars, leaving her with nothing but the sense of having ignored a powerful warning of imminent and pressing danger.

THE FIRST NIGHT

She couldn't sleep. Last night, cramped in sardine-class as they flew over the sub-continent, Miranda had longed to lie down, to stretch out, to be comfortable. She could neither read nor sleep. She had even envied Jim, relaxed beside her, happily absorbed in *A Compendium of Aircraft Crashes*. And now here she was, in a vast king size bed, Jim snoring gently beside her, and she was wide awake.

She could go for a walk round the island. That might be soothing. The islands were lovely at night. She looked at her watch. 1.15! Yes, she would have to do something to while away the hours before Jim's alarm clock went off. It would whirr loudly at about 5.30, so that he would be all set for a pre-dawn dive, before the real day's diving started.

She rolled carefully off the bed. The marble floor felt slippery under her feet, and almost cool, thanks to the efforts of the ceiling fan. There were a few ants in the bathroom, and something larger and more cockroachy putting itself discreetly behind the mirror. Don't bother me and I won't bother you, Miranda promised, looking at her undefended feet.

The bathroom was a bonus, all in marble, with a wonderful arrangement whereby there was only half a roof, so that tropical plants grew inside the room, and they could look up at coconut palms while sitting on the loo. The glass was cunningly tilted so that the rain wouldn't fall on the occupant of the toilet seat, but would be channelled into the surprising flowerbed that flourished inside the room. Yellow and white oleander flowers nodded cheerfully at scarlet hibiscus. Brilliant. Why didn't all bathrooms have flowers growing in them? It meant the room

3

was always steamy hot too. No cold chills, or cold tiles under their feet when they had their shower.

The small island had been a pleasant surprise altogether. Their party of divers had been met at the little jetty by smiling white-coated staff with tall, cool glasses of lime juice, perfectly sweetened. Then hot scented flannels had been offered round while they waited to check in. It had been wonderful to get some of the stickiness of travel off. Jim had got his villa near the Dive Shop as requested, so they were on the other side of the island from Reception, which meant a whole five minutes' walk to the restaurant.

The villas were set at intervals around the edge of the island so that everyone had their own stretch of beach. And there were two shops. There was the little utilitarian Postcards And Things You Have Forgotten To Pack Shop; and a pretty marble room selling island artefacts, which included a tiny beauty salon. There was even a library/reading room next to them. It was a small office with a fan, a television, and a shelf of bodice rippers. They were mainly in German, but there was also a set of alarming comic books in Japanese. Miranda hoped she would be noble and donate all her holiday books to the island at the end of their week; it was about time an English shelf got started. She had bought Janet Frame's three-part autobiography with her on this holiday and was longing to get started on it. Maybe, one day, she would be able to donate a copy of her own novel, if it ever got written. Her recent success with a series of articles about the expatriate life had got everyone telling her that she ought to write a book. A thriller. A potential Hollywood blockbuster.

Jim took a party of scuba divers to a small tropical island every year, so, if it was possible to write a novel on holiday, that could be a production rate of a book a year. But what on earth to write about? And who?

The island air was as hot and wet as the warm, scented flannels they had been greeted with. It smelt of the frangipani blossom that covered it. These were towering frangipani trees, not the bushes of their expat home. Here pot plants grew to giant size. But the villa – one room with marbled bathroom – felt wonderfully cool.

They had both spent ages in the bathroom, under its Niagara of a showerhead built for two. There was hot water aplenty. It felt like sweet water too. Not sieved seawater such as they had in their company villas but real water, although drinking water had to be bought in bottles from the bar. Which gave the male half of Jim's shoal of divers the perfect excuse. It was cheaper to drink the beer.

Perhaps she should have had a beer or two and then she might have been sleeping as soundly as Jim, Miranda regretted, as she tiptoed out of the bathroom, keeping a wary eye on the large golden cockroach, which seemed to be watching her just as intently from behind the mirror. Perhaps there was a whole gang of cockroaches inside their little hide – all watching her through binoculars? 'It's a Red-Haired Miranda!' they'd be exclaiming geekishly. 'Its colours are fading and it's past its prime', as they ticked her off in their People-Spotting albums.

Yes, they were a middle-aged shoal of divers these days. And, as they grew older and larger, it seemed that their yearly tropical islands grew smaller and younger. This one was in its very first tourist season, and Jim's Shoal were among its first divers ever. Surely, if there was a thriller to be extracted from these dive holidays, it should have been written way back then, when they were all younger and more adventurous.

And in those days she had slept soundly. But now she had slipped completely out of sleep mode. There was nothing for it but a walk round the moonlit island.

Miranda jumped as something scuffled and pattered on the chalet roof. Something small. Rats, the boys would say, hoping to startle the girls. But she thought it was the flying foxes out a' hunting in the moonlight.

5

She slipped on sandals and her light robe, got the key from Jim's bedside table and locked the villa door behind her. There were signs up all over the islands now, even this one, so innocent and new, warning you about locking the door, not leaving bags unattended, and all the rest of it – a reminder that the serpent was still in the garden.

Miranda would walk along the white sand, cool in the moonlight, and watch the light on the water, the phosphorescent fish moving to the perfect rhythm of their shoals. She would splash along the water's edge in her sandals. Jim always advised against going barefoot into the water here. Even the shells could be deadly. No. However lovely it looked, it wasn't Paradise.

She stepped through the mangrove and frangipani that laced the edge of the island, but found no beach. Only a silver moon glinting on restless silver water. The tide was really high. It was just a few feet from their front door. Perhaps the island beaches had got smaller? Jim thought that the beach on Last Year's Island had shrunk since the time he and the Shoal first visited it. But Mal the Dentist didn't think so.

So was this just the usual high tide? Did you get tides so near the Equator? Miranda tried to reach back to the geography lessons of her faraway convent schooldays, but nothing helpful emerged from storage.

She would have to walk round on the inner path. The luggage path. She tiptoed through the sandy space between the villas, having to sidestep to avoid the vicious little thorny plants that had somehow got loose on the island. They would be rounded up and exterminated when the early morning gardeners began their rounds.

The stars were shining brightly – full of joy. The moon was startling, appearing through gaps in the trees, silvering the path in front of her, disappearing behind a drift of cloud, then lighting her way again. And the silence! There was just the beat of the sea against the island edges, murmuring behind the circle of chalets. She would walk past Reception, round to the Dive shop and back to their villa.

She looked at the face of her watch in the moonlight. It was funny how different time was at night. 1.30 in the afternoon had a certain feel to it, and a colour – a kind of beige perhaps? It signalled a long stretch of boredom in Miranda's department, with all the hot hours of the desert afternoon still to come. And here the hands of her watch were in exactly the same place, but it was a different feeling altogether. This was an immeasurable time. The next hour could be as long as a night, or slip away unnoticed in her dreams.

And she would sleep. She was determined. The gentle crash of the waves on the sand was so relaxing, even though she worried that the sea was nibbling and eating at the edge of the island. Miranda wondered if there were rabbits on this island too. Last year there had been a few on their bigger island. She had enjoyed being able to feed them after dinner. She and the other girls would bring carrots and lettuce from the salad buffet.

Something was rustling in the undergrowth alongside her, or beside her. It was hard to tell. There would be fruit bats here of course, and some birds – and scuttles of crabs. The worried face of the moon looked down, glowing in the night sky. You might well look worried, moon, Miranda sympathised. You can see just what we are doing to the earth. But above you, the stars maintain their joy. And they see much further than you do.

The ocean beat on as the bushes stirred beside her. Miranda thought of Chessman, their fierce Arabian cat. How he would follow her and Jim on their walks, keeping as close as a dog would. He would love it here, rustling through the undergrowth after her. What would he make of the hermit crabs? Probably, knowing Chess, he would be rather unkind to them. Unless the first one he met gave his nose a good sharp pinch. In which case he would simply pretend that they were beneath his notice.

When she was away, she missed Chess. And she felt guilty for leaving him. He was her baby, since Emily left.

But there were always the fish to feed. At Last Year's Island, there had been shoals of baby sharks that hung round in the water under the dining hall bridge, turning upside down and savaging their toast crumbs with great charm. Yes, she would surely find fish to feed. And birds. And maybe rabbits. And she would have the pleasure of seven days away from housework and the department. She would have time to read and write. She was no diver – she came for the peace and beauty of the islands. Especially at night.

Miranda jumped again as the undergrowth beside her rustled and splashed suddenly. That couldn't have been a wave! Not this side of the villas! The polar caps weren't melting that fast. She decided to try for the beach again. And, yes, near Reception there was a sliver of clear silver sand, enough to walk along. Now she could watch the soothing sea, and the moon on the water. The rustling was on the other side of her now. Almost like some animal that had splashed out of the sea in panic at her approach. She must remember to ask Jim if there was anything here that could do that. Miranda yawned. She would pretend it was Chess, here with her in spirit, if not the flesh.

There was a whirring noise in her ear, and a large golden cockroach flew past. She wondered if it was the little chap from their bathroom. The tropics were so insecty. She yawned again. Sleep was beginning to seem a real possibility. She would count Chessmen as she walked round, and see if that helped.

The hypnotic waves, and the rustlings and purrings of Chess did their work. By the time No 32 began to come round again, Miranda's eyes were closing. It was getting darker, and she stumbled a little, getting a sharp jab from something thorny growing by the path. Those wretched little bushes. They were not very user-friendly things to find here, on Paradise Island. The clouds were thickening now. Perhaps they would have rain. On the best trips it rained torrentially, but at night. So that by the morning all was fresh and clear and sunny. The Shoal required sunny days on holiday, despite having three hundred and sixty four days of unrelenting sunshine in their desert town. This was a puzzle to Miranda.

Now she could hear the rain pattering quickly after her, drowning out … what? Nothing. Just wind on the water, wind in the crackly clumps of bamboos. The door of No 32, fragrant with frangipani, swam into view, and Miranda, forgetting the large rustlings of the sea, and the small rustlings of the land, tucked herself in next to Jim and fell into a deep and dreamless sleep.

THE FIRST DAY

'No. Just throw the yolks away.' Exasperated. 'He doesn't get it.' Mal was starting off his morning with some nicely raised blood pressure.

The American part of the Shoal had the omelette cooks on their usual islands trained. The yolks were thrown away. Not a speck must taint the white omelettes that they required. But the Small Island cook was having trouble understanding. Miranda saw Jim weigh in to sort it out – and then hover round to make sure he got the traditional version.

Had anyone got the Brit character off as well as Australians have, with their whingeing Pom jokes, wondered Miranda, as she watched the British half of the Shoal stoically accept whatever the cook chose to give them, and then grumble about it back at their tables. The cook on Last Year's Island was much more efficient, apparently. How strange it was of Jim to change the venue this year. And … Oh Hi, Jimbo, we're having a great time. Thumbs up, mate.

It was funny the confusion it could cause in a mixed group, with the Americans being so can-do. They assumed that if things were being whinged about, then things ought to be fixed. They understood nothing about the pleasures of aimless whingeing. Which did make them good holiday companions.

Miranda looked round at the splendid breakfast bar. This was a long way from fish and the odd coconut. It was as good, if not better, as anything on the larger islands that lay near the mainland. There was even a special Japanese section for the divers who were sharing the island with them.

I shall watch how they do it and have a go myself tomorrow, thought

Miranda, who found all the little bowls and shapes intriguing. It followed a slightly courtly pattern, a breakfast ritual in which you had to know the steps. Miranda was depressed by the way formality and courtliness was being drained out of the world, and found the Japanese breakfast dance reassuring.

I don't think I'll have the raw fish though. And definitely not anything that you have to stir a raw egg into. And, in the meantime … In front of her was a good choice of cereals, fresh yoghurt in a bowl, and fruit juice. There was the coconut, nicely cut. But there were also pineapple, apples, and some little slices of passion fruit. And now the hot table. Quite a feast! Scrambled eggs. Pallid sausages. Potato cakes. Baked beans. Bacon! Or rather the same version of it they had in their expat homeland. Oh, and a dahl, simmering quietly away in its silver salver. And even a fish curry.

Dahl then, with yoghurt. And a chapatti from the towering tray that had just arrived. And a nice hot cup of tea. Their waiter had appeared the instant they got to the large table set aside for the Shoal, and offered a choice of tea or coffee. The tea was good. Hot, strong and freshly made. They were close to the home of tea here.

'Can we have some toast, please?' Jim had arrived with his omelette

He looked panicky as the waiter disappeared. 'Oh no. I forgot …' But Miranda was already rummaging through the enormous handbag that accompanied her everywhere, and she pulled out Golden Shred marmalade and HP sauce with the flourish of a stage magician.

'Ah, brilliant. Thanks.' They smiled at each other, and he settled down happily to his breakfast.

'Miranda, what are you eating!' That was Inga and Alison arriving. Inga hadn't been on a Jim trip before.

Miranda did her usual explanations and sat through the usual exclamations about eating curry for breakfast. Who decreed that eggs and boiled sausages weren't strange, but bread, beans and yoghurt were?

And why was omelette and HP sauce alright? On a tropical island, where the keeping of hens was an improbability, and there wasn't an HP sauce bush for a thousand miles? Ah, but why shudder at raw fish and raw eggs at any hour of the day then, her conscience asked.

'You're up early. You didn't do the morning dive did you?'

'You have to be joking.' That was Alison. 'We aren't signed up for any dives today. We're going to snorkel off the house reef. And then lie on the beach. We all meant to sleep in. But we couldn't sleep. Well, Inga and I couldn't. I don't know about Diane.'

'No, neither could I. Isn't it maddening, all that time on the plane and I longed to lie down. And then when I got to bed, I was completely awake. Jim was fine though. Slept like a log.' Miranda was surprised to register that Diane wasn't sharing with them. She was sure that they had been down as a threesome on the list. She probably ought to make some exclamation of surprise and ask where she was. But, truthfully, she felt it none of her business.

'So what are your plans for today?'

'Well …' Miranda hesitated. She intended to use this holiday to proofread the article about expat life she had sold and make a start on her proposed thriller. It was to be geared for the current market, and about expats. According to her agent it would be much easier to sell if she could manage a Hollywood style heroine. She would have to be tough and feisty, with a permanent tan, a tiny waist, a large chest, and vast bottom-kicking abilities. Though definitely not a vast bottom.

And, right on cue, a heroine had arrived uninvited in her mind, on the plane. She was a sort of uber Miranda. Carmen Miranda perhaps? But a lady not at all like her beautiful predecessor, who was from an age when Hollywood had glamour and beauty. This Carmen had kept threatening to fly the plane herself, to wallop any possible hijackers, and to keep her hair big and glossy at all times. She had followed them to the island, and was obviously going to be very annoying.

Why did women have to be so tough in fiction? Why couldn't they be wimps occasionally and take it easy? And sometimes have small hair.

'I'm going to tackle my paperwork. So you will find me on the patio, correcting proofs.' Because I don't want to shop. I don't want to gossip about workmates we have left behind us. I just want to sit and soak in the calm, fresh beauty of Small Island. And do a little bit of work. Because, if I can only do a little better moneywise with my writing, I can give up the department. So, thought guilty, unsociable Miranda, please don't find me.

THE FIRST DIVE

'Small Island. Well, it does what it says on the tin. It really is small.'

Breakfast was over, and Miranda was on the jetty with the Pats –
Patrick and Patricia – watching the dive boat loading up. They were
already kitted out for the dive, looking lean and photogenic, which was
quite an achievement for expats in dive suits. None of them were that
young anymore. Trish really was gorgeous. They both were. Patrick tall
and lean and fair, and Trish tall and dark and tanned. They were talking
about the name of the island, which was very long, and ended in 'vili'.
They had decided that it meant 'Small Island'.

'Small Island! What a mercy it isn't Big Island then, or it would take
all week just to say the name!' That was Patrick.

'It's smaller than any of the other islands I've been to.' That was
Miranda. It hadn't occurred to her to think anything much about the
island's name, beyond that it was a pretty word in its native dress.

'On no, it's exciting, I asked Mo last night.' Trish and her various island
waiters usually became penfriends. 'He went very quiet, and then he
leaned over, he didn't exactly whisper, but quiet you know, and said it
means The Island Where Something Small …'

'Come on Trish, we'll start without you.' The Shoal was impatient to
be off.

Miranda thought of the small rustlings in the night bushes. She waved
till they disappeared beyond the house reef, the matter of islands and their
names melting carelessly from her mind in the heat. The boat was almost
full for the first morning. Only Inga and Alison didn't go. Diane went with
Mal. Which enlightened Miranda as to where she was actually sleeping.

15

Mal and Diane! Diane was small, skinny and boyish, and Miranda had pinpointed the tall, tanned and shapely Inga as the girl for Mal.

Anyway, that was their business. Not hers. The Company Town they lived in was gossipy enough, but Miranda lived right at the end of the grapevine. Which she didn't mind as she found it was usually more cheering not to know too much about what was going on. Expats had a lot of time on their hands, as so much was done for them. Some used that time wisely, but some did not.

'The devil finds work for idle hands to do' had been one of the maxims of her faraway childhood. So who knows what goes on? Certainly not me, admitted Miranda. She watched the hermit crabs busy shopping for shell around their mangrove bushes, and sighed and turned back to her empty notebook. She needed one simple idea to build her plot round … without the tiresome Carmen if possible. A crab scuttled on to the patio, stared at an ant, and, finding it useless shell-wise, scuttled off again. Now if those were spiders, even half as big, I simply couldn't come here, Miranda thought. And she wondered why scuttling crabs were OK, but scuttling spiders were toe curling.

What was it scuttling about for? Food as well as shell, she supposed. And the ant didn't really serve in either capacity.

This was an island where lots of small things scuttled about. Perhaps that was what the long name ending in 'vili' meant. She found herself thinking again about all they had left on their plates at breakfast. The half-eaten sausages and omelettes. How did it all get here – so far away in the Indian Ocean. Chessman, their desert cat, would have wolfed it down. Miranda hoped that the staff went round with doggy bags afterwards, collected it all up and fed the reef fish with it. Such a waste otherwise.

Carmen Miranda stayed away. You couldn't connect her with food at all. She probably just topped herself up at the nearest silicon pump every now and then.

16

Miranda decided that if she was going to write something, she must start now and do an hour or so every morning. After all, her location could hardly be more exotic. And here were her expats – her raw material. Or, at any rate, they were out there in the Indian Ocean just next door. What a setting for a successful, filmable thriller. A setting for what though? Something sizzling about expat life?

But she and Jim didn't really have sizzle. They had a routine. A boring routine no doubt, to anyone else but them. Jim went off to the school each day and taught. He came home each evening and taught diving. Then they had a glass of something home brewed on their flower filled patio with whichever friends had stopped by, watched a bit of telly, and went to bed.

Miranda went to work in Media three days a week. Which sounded glamorous enough, but all she was doing was filing and typing. Everything required a form. And forms had to be typed and filed. And that is what she did. Where was the potential in that? Carmen herself couldn't make anything glamorous out of it.

I suppose she could be a feisty secretary, exposing the scandal of how … Miranda yawned. If the thought of it bored even its author, then what was the point of going on with the idea?

They had had some wonderful holidays together – them and the shoal of expat divers. But wonderful in the Carmen Miranda sense? Filmable wonderful? None of Jim's divers had ever yet been eaten by a giant shark, hell bent on revenge for something or other. Nor had any comets fallen into the water anywhere in the Shoal's vicinity, and, mercifully, the skyscraper hotels they sometimes stayed in were not in the habit of catching fire. They just dove. And ate. And had a laugh. And spent time in the bar.

Film-of-the-book notwithstanding, Miranda could only hope it stayed that way. A Jim dive holiday was always fun, it always went well. And this was shaping up to be their loveliest island yet – so lovely that it was impossible to concentrate this first morning. Within half an hour the beauty of the coral sea had pulled her through the mangroves and out on to the tiny white sand beach in front of their villa – 'their beach'. The sea lay beyond, breathtaking in its blues and turquoises. It was not so calm today. There was a large swell beyond the protective ring of the reef. Their chalet placed them at the fattest part of the lagoon, with the broad channel to the ocean right opposite.

I'll swim, decided Miranda. It's too lovely not to. And, for the moment, she would have the whole lagoon to herself. The island was emptying. It looked like the Japanese party was leaving. She had heard the sound of cases being dragged along the inner ring road earlier. The next boatload of holidaymakers wouldn't be shipped in till the afternoon, so for the moment the island belonged to Miranda, the Shoal, and the staff.

The afternoon divers would be from Germany. She knew that because Gordo was arriving with them. She was glad Gordo was coming. He was one of Jim's regular dive buddies. They dove together all over the world. And Gordo was infinitely patient with the photography, which meant a lot of hanging around underwater.

Miranda waded into the warm bath of the lagoon, thinking rather enviously of the glossy blondes on the holiday brochures. She herself came in two (un)lovely colourways: corpse white, or lobster red. But thinking about that brought the impeccably tanned and siliconed Carmen roaring back, speedboating across the lagoon in a stylish way.

Miranda had no wish for her company, not even in her planned thriller, so she stopped thinking, rocked comfortably by the swell in the warm water of the Indian Ocean. Although the water was surging over the reef top, it seemed to die quietly on the small white beach, without any particular drama of waves, as if the sea was being tender with such a baby island.

Miranda swam right out over the reef to its edge. Suddenly there was nothing beneath her, just an endless fall. The lagoon had been like a cosy room, shutting out this cold and not so user-friendly ocean. She trod water and looked back at the island. She could see it all from here. It was only a few million years since it had been born from the ocean, so it was barely past the toddler stage. But it was already thickly wooded with tropical vegetation and columned with curving coconut palms. It had all its hair.

The creatures that had rustled in the night slept somewhere in there. The sand was back from its night excursions and ringed the island in pure white. Around it was the glowing green lagoon with its intermittent frills and beyond that was the bright blue Indian Ocean. Somewhere underneath that ocean were Jim and the Shoal.

Miranda pulled her goggles over her eyes and stared down the wall of the reef, seeing what the divers would be seeing. Comical striped clown fish swarmed below her. They were bold little things, with their big brother anemones to look after them, and they would dart out at her if she got too near their home. Oh, and there was a pipefish. And a parrot fish. Miranda thought that they were perhaps the most beautiful fish of all. They were painted in shining colours with a delicate and skilful brush. Jim said that sometimes, underwater, it was possible to hear their beaks crunching on the reef. Oh, and there was the gorgeous vacuum cleaner of the reef, the sea slug.

It's as if I've gone through the looking-glass, thought Miranda. I have made it back through the gates of Paradise, through that little door that Alice saw, when she was too big to get in. And then, when she got small, like our island, she didn't have the key. The key to Paradise. But how to find it? Have we found it here?

The swell sucked at her and bounced her nearer the reef. The coral, lovely, but sharp and often poisonous, was best not touched. And things lurked on it that looked like coral, but weren't. They were definitely best not touched. Surely there should be nothing poisonous in Paradise, nothing thorny?

She swam lazily along the edge watching the fish. Curious and confident, they would often come right up to her. Where will my fish-feeding station be this time, she wondered. I must remember to pop down to that jetty by the dining hall with some lunchtime rolls and see what I can find.

The swell was getting bigger, rolling her around in a relaxing way. She looked into the depths below her, fading into a murkiness that could hide anything. She remembered the fierce little baby sharks of Last Year's Island, savaging the breakfast toast crumbs with such charm. Perhaps she ought to swim back over the reef and into the lagoon whose sandy bottom hid no secrets? But the mention of 'bottom' threatened to bring Carmen back, in kicking mood. Miranda made her way cautiously over the main reef, but the sea had got so big it swept her safely over without touching anything. Now, so much nearer the shore, she could relax and not worry about what might be underneath. She began to stroke slowly towards the white beach. Those little sharks, with their baby teeth … A large shadow floated under her. Or rather I floated over it, she told herself. It's just an outcropping from the reef, which had scattered bits of itself all over the lagoon. But an unwelcome idea had drifted into her mind.

Babies mean parents, somewhere. But not in the lagoon. There were only small fish in lagoons. But there were many sharks of all sizes in the Indian Ocean just metres away from her. She looked back. She was halfway between reef edge and shore now. The water was still pouring over the top of the coral causing the lagoon to fill and swell and surge softly on to its beach. But surely that swell wouldn't provide enough space for a big shark to get over the reef top? Surely not. Just how deep was it?

Suddenly she remembered the channel out to the ocean. How deep would it be today with this fierce sea outside? She found she didn't want to go back and find out. Another shadow. She drew her legs up hastily, put on her goggles, and looked into the waters underneath. It was just another large patch of coral. The reef outcropped all over the place. There were fish everywhere, lovely speckled blue and red and banded orange. All the colours of the rainbow under here. And the deep saturated red and orange sponges. Blood red. Blood orange. Although didn't Jim say that blood was green underwater? If you swam deep enough. How on earth did he know that?

Miranda hoped that there wasn't a Carmen Miranda moment coming up. If only the large pieces of reef down there in the water would stay in one place. The swelling water almost made it seem ... she swam more strongly and soon found herself much nearer the beach and swimming fast.

Isn't the rule with sharks that if you leave them alone, they will leave you alone, hoped Miranda, remembering her pact with the Bathroom Cockroach. But perhaps she was bothering them by simply being here. And with such an empty lagoon she was the only target, if ... if ... if she had felt something brush by her. Vaguely she wondered why Inga and Alison weren't swimming too. Perhaps they were round the other side of the island.

The swell kept pulling her back, but suddenly her knees bumped into sand. She had hit the sloping shelf of the beach. She let her legs down gingerly and waded thankfully through the shallows, not stopping until she hit dry sand – and flopped down, feeling foolish.

She seemed to have some red sponge on her foot. That was careless. You should never touch the reef or the things of the reef. It doesn't do the reef any good.

And it doesn't do you any good, because, look, she had blood on her foot. Green blood, shining red above water. I must have caught myself on one of those sharp outcrops after all, Miranda thought. And I was so careful.

Suddenly her foot was burning and throbbing. That was quite a gash. To add to the thorn slashes of last night! Better get back to the chalet and disinfect and cover it up. Things quickly went bad in the tropics. She limped off through the mangroves, leaving the beach and lagoon to themselves, and soon the waves swept up and washed away her footprints with their drops of rust, cleaning the baby island as they had done since the day it was born.

AFTER THE DIVE

The Shoal – the first trip on the dive boat always welded them into a shoal – met up again at lunchtime. They had a large round table set out for them, looking across the glittering waters and the jetty where they had arrived on Small Island yesterday. They had had a successful morning, although the current had been strong, and Todd had been sick because of the swell – or more likely because of his previous night's exploits at happy hour. But they had been to the marvellous coral gardens of Banana Point, and there was a possibility of manta rays in the afternoon.

'We've been lucky with the weather too', Jim pointed out, in between mouthfuls of freshly caught reef fish. 'We just got a swell, apparently the mainland had a tropical storm. If the Japanese hadn't left so early, they wouldn't have got off the island at all. I don't know what will have happened at the other end, whether their plane got in or not. I half expected to find them all back here, on the island.'

'And guaranteed mantas this afternoon?' That was Mal arriving with an enormous plateful of steak, onion gravy and fries.

'Well, they've already been seen at the Point, and apparently the currents are right this afternoon.' Patrick had steak too, along with fries and fish.

'I reckon we will see them,' said Jim, through another mouthful of fish, 'even if not today.'

'The current this morning was bad.' Trish arrived, with her vast plate of salad. She had salad at lunchtime, so that she could have two goes at the dessert trolley every evening.

It seemed to work as she maintained a slim athletic figure. She also managed a year round tan that didn't fade or change.

The words: 'You should have come with us, Miranda,' were hovering above them in the ether, waiting for someone to pull them down.

'You should have come with us Miranda.' It was Diane who actually said it. Miranda had to explain it every year. She didn't grudge Jim his dive holidays, just grudged constantly having to explain herself. A change of subject usually helped. She would go out on the dive boat once. And once only.

'This soup is lovely.'

'Yes' – good old Patrick – 'It's never seen a packet, I can assure you of that. And have you seen that dessert table?!'

Yes. And it's only lunchtime, thought Miranda. Whatever will we have tonight? Her foot was hurting where she had gashed it. It was going to become more and more irritating as the days wore on. She hoped it wouldn't put a stop to her night walks round the island. She thought of Jim's first trips to these island archipelagos. He had been passionate about the islands ever since his first visit many years ago. They had roughed it in those days. Him and Gordo and Wolfie. And sometimes Mal. They had lived off coconuts, and rice and what fish they could catch. They had slept in the dhonis, their standard dive boats, and bathed in lagoons.

'Eat all you want.' Jim was happily clearing his enormous plateload. 'This afternoon's dive is going to be hard work.'

'But worth it. For mantas?' Diane had found the currents of the vast ocean alarming.

'Remember when we were at Sipadan, and the mantas were feeding for days.'

Miranda felt relieved as the diving conversation took off and left her behind. She set about her plate of salad – such a wonderful selection on the buffet, even fresh asparagus – and got lost in her own thoughts. The ocean was like a jewel beside them, and the dining room, open on all sides, caught a small refreshing breeze that assisted the slowly turning fans.

When she saw beauty like this, it made Miranda wonder why. And wonder how. She also wondered about the fresh asparagus and how far it had to travel to get here.

'Hiya.' Inga and Alison arrived, both with helpings of soup and salad. 'Is anyone having wine, or shall we wait till dinner?'

Jim, whose mouth was full of dessert, waved his beer at them, and they settled for a bottle of water.

They were all gathered apart from Todd. He was still feeling sick. But he was probably not going to socialize as a Shoalie. He would have his own concerns, Miranda felt. He really didn't like expat women, or most probably any women at all, and those who had taken up with him suffered for it.

Unnecessarily, Miranda felt. If someone has a wife – or a husband – then leave them alone. Or don't expect it will turn out well if you don't. Didn't people once used to understand those rules? They may have often broken them, ever since Adam and Eve decided perfection wasn't for them, but surely people used to realize that there would be consequences?

She had met Marie-Terese, Todd's wife, once, during a dive trip to the Philippines. She was very lovely of course, but tough too. No fragile lotus blossom she. And she suited Todd well, or so Miranda thought. They suited each other. Marie-Terese had a shrewd eye for business and money. And Todd financed things for her, and educated her teenage daughter from some previous liaison. Together they made money. And she provided him with his alibi. He could always, at the last minute, if necessary, wriggle out of anything that looked like commitment via a conveniently faraway wife. It wasn't Romeo and Juliet. But what was in this world? The thought of Todd as a stepfather to a daughter was a depressing one. Miranda could only hope she was as tough as her mother.

Miranda sighed for what was and for what ought to be, because out here it seemed as if the paint of creation still glistened as freshly as if they were in the perfect morning of the world. They were bathed in frangipani fragrance and ocean breeze. Scarlet hibiscus nodded softly at them. Coconut palms fed and shaded them. The gem-like ocean held a million different living jewels and the sun had thoughtfully gilded some of the palm fronds, leaving reminders of its golden self even in the shadows.

If there is a Paradise, here it is. And yet ... Something must have gone horribly wrong, somewhere. Something small. Just a small piece of fruit, Eve. What harm can it do?

Everyone was telling Alison and Inga what a great dive they had missed. But they were able to retaliate with tales of the house reef moray eel and its babies.

Inga was certain that she had seen the mother eel chasing other fish off from her little wrigglers – protecting them and caring for them as a mother should. Apparently this was against all the textbooks. But, to Miranda, thinking of their faraway Emily, nothing seemed more likely.

'Gordo should be here this afternoon. He'll arrive with the German divers.'

'Will he go out on the boat with you?'

'No. He won't be in time. It leaves at 2.15 prompt. And anyway, he has to do his check-out dive before they'll let him out for the serious stuff. Pity though.' Jim longed to have his dive buddy back.

'2.15!' Mal leapt up, leaving his plateload of creamy puddings untouched. 'I'm outta here. I've got to get my cameras sorted.' Jim always remarked that people didn't listen to instructions. But that didn't usually include Mal. He must have his mind on something else, Miranda concluded. Lovesick, perhaps? Diane disappeared in Mal's wake, closely followed by Alison and Inga, and the rest of the Shoal, until Jim and Miranda were left alone, sitting over the cup of tea with which they finished every meal.

Whatever happened to all the leftovers, Miranda wondered once again. None of them had even finished what was on their plates, never mind what was left on the generous buffet tables. 'Your eyes are bigger than your stomachs,' she seemed to hear her mother say. Although it would take pretty large eyes to compete with some expat stomachs.

'It's two o'clock Jim. We'd better be getting back.'

'Five more minutes. I put all my stuff on the boat before we came for lunch. Just a quick trip to the loo, and I'll be ready.'

They strolled off hand in hand, going up central – their just discovered short cut through the centre of the island where the staff lived. And past the little palace they had found there.

'That's for the air hostesses, right?'

'No. I was asking Wolfie. It's for Mr Al-Auddin. He's the owner of this island. He and his wives stay here sometimes.'

'Al-Auddin. That would be of *his lamp* fame? Wow. But why is it in the middle of the island? Why not on the beach?'

'I expect the wives are all in purdah or something.'

Yes, probably thought Miranda. That's why it has such high white walls, with narrow grilled gates at the front. So narrow that not even a mouse could creep through. Miranda peeped in. And got a tempting glimpse of gardens, bright flowers and a fountain. A paradise within a paradise.

'I wonder if he's here this week. I'd love to see inside. Do you think he lets us tourists in?'

But Jim was looking serious. And Miranda stopped talking, leaving him to muse on whether or not he had packed exactly the right lenses for the manta ray trip.

So they were on an island owned by Aladdin, of all those wonderful childhood stories. Who knows what might happen next?

AFTERNOON

The Lord of the Island was either away, or his power was not yet being felt, because the afternoon progressed as these dive trip afternoons always did. Miranda waved the Shoal off at the jetty, wishing Jim a safe trip – and manta rays aplenty – although if they did see mantas, Gordo would be upset to have missed them. After she limped back to their villa and put some more soothing stuff on her leg, Inga, Alison and Diane turned up on her veranda. Diane had had enough diving for one day. She wasn't at all keen on the ocean currents. Miranda put her proofs to one side. She longed to ask about Mal, and how long he and Diane had been together.

She, personally, thought Mal was gorgeous. A nice guy too. A fun guy. And he was single! Long divorced. That wasn't a combination single girls came across every day of the week, especially not in Expatland. He worked in the company dental hospital, on the American payroll. So money was no problem either.

On the other hand, Mal had two marriages and five children behind him. And, with the best will in the world, that made things complicated. As if picking her thoughts out of the air, Diane began to tell them how upset Mal had been that she wasn't going on the afternoon dive with him. 'That's the problem with us. He wants me with him all the time. I don't get any space. I feel I can't breathe sometimes.' Miranda felt that Alison wanted to say something on the lines of, 'Hey, Mal can get in my space any time!' but had restrained herself.

Why?

Was it because she didn't want them to be together? Didn't she want to paint Mal as attractive as he undoubtedly was? Or was it simply that she thought it would be tactless? Could anyone honestly say that Alison was noted for her tact? Diane lay back on the swing seat, rocking gently as they watched her. She was so tiny she fitted in neatly end to end. She would have to wear immensely high heels, if she and six foot Mel were ever to walk down the aisle together.

Yet her way of talking wasn't at all animated, thought Miranda, quite forgetting to make a mental note of the actual dialogue. She spoke a sort of flat Essex. And she was really a bit too thin for short shorts. If one can be too thin nowadays? In Carmen Miranda's world somebody's rear end would have received a sharp kicking for such a thought-crime.

'Gil won't commit. He just won't. And I'm tired of it, I told him.'

Alison had been putting the case for Gil – someone Miranda had assumed was by now one of Diane's many ex-boyfriends. In fact, she had thought it was the trauma of their latest 'final' bust up that had propelled Diane out here, to get over it.

'Well, if you can make something of it, see some future in it.' That was Inga, doubtful. But she was apparently neutral in this, with no agenda. Something – some kind of happiness, thought Miranda – had made her uncomplicated. It was as if she had moved from the world of Expat Singlegirldom into a mistier place, one that required less alertness and strategy.

'Yes, but you know you can't break up with Gil. How many times have you tried?'

Alison seemed to have some vested interest in the Gil Diane relationship.

Miranda thought that if she did have any of this intuition that all women were supposed to possess by the bucket-load, she would know why. Alison never usually had a good word to say about Gil. Nor he about her. Could it be because there was no future in it, and so Alison would get her best friend back safe and sound?

'I know, but now there's Mal. And I mean ...' She was indignant, her voice as heated as Diane's voice could ever get. 'You know where Gil's gone.'

Obviously they did, although Miranda didn't. The subsequent discussions revealed that he had selfishly gone back to spend a month with his wife and children.

After they had left her, and drifted off towards their chalets or the beach, Miranda thought over the conversation. Yet again a change had come about, while she was in her expat sleep. You met the new intake of incomers from your homeland, your people, your tribe. But they were different. None of the girls had made marriage an issue. Gil's marriage that is. There was no moral hesitation, no feeling that it might perhaps be wrong to go out with a married man – and one with young children at that.

Gil was gorgeous. He had a good job. For a Brit within their company, he was a high earner. And presumably, the only imperative was: if it feels good, do it. Miranda had sensed there was a feeling that Diane was being foolish, wasting her precious time, because he would never leave his wife. But beyond that, nothing. How did that change come about? When did the knowledge of the sacredness of marriage vanish from people's minds?

What would people regard as bad now? Morally wrong?

Eating a cream cake, or a bar of chocolate? Yes, to do that would qualify as bad. Just as refraining from eating it would mean you had been good. She could imagine any of them saying: 'I've been really bad today, I had one of those cream desserts, and some chips with my fish!' What she could not imagine them saying was: 'I've been really bad over the last few months, I've been going out with a married man and trying to persuade him to leave his wife and young children and marry me.'

So if Diane's liaison with Gil was frowned on, it was only because he likely wouldn't get that divorce. Although Miranda hadn't said so, she thought he would leave his wife. But not yet. And not for Diane. And in the meantime, Mrs Gil and the kids, safely back in England, provided him with the perfect excuse for playing the field, while not 'committing'. Was he just the Brit version of Todd?

So here would be a subject for a first novel. Surely there was a whole series waiting up there in the ether somewhere? Bridget Jones Goes to Work in Expatland and Writes a Diary? Sally Potter and the Expats' Moan?

No. The only thing that could be said for them was there was no role for her dreadful alter ego Carmen Miranda in it. Miranda sighed. Whichever way she looked at it, writing about her ghastly heroine was going to be no fun at all.

Should she come at it from another angle? If she was one of those Victorian writers, a Mrs Henry Wood say, how would she write about these things? In fact, what would she write about, full stop? The moral dilemmas that preoccupied the Mrs Wood heroines no longer existed. Miranda tried to imagine Diane wondering what God might have to say about the Gil/Mal liaisons. But it was unimaginable.

And could she work, say, Carmen Miranda into East Lynne? If she did, the rather pallid hero, Mr Carlisle, wouldn't know what had hit him. Although it would in fact be Carmen's size nine foot connecting with his rump – and the novel would be over in five minutes.

What sort of world would she find the next time she and Jim went back 'home'?

She lay on her bed, her proofs scattered beside her. The girls had left for their first appointment at the very expensive if tiny Beauty Shop. The afternoon heat pressed down, saturating everything. The fan swung round and round, shifting the hot wet air sluggishly. She could turn the air con on, but that meant moving, getting off the bed, trekking across the floor to the switch by the bathroom. And, twenty minutes later, trekking back again to shut off the blast of icy air that was beginning make her teeth chatter.

Now Miranda found herself worrying about falling asleep. If she did, she would be out for hours. And she would miss the boats arriving with all the newcomers. And Jim wanted her to be at the jetty to meet Gordo. But the bed was so comfy, the room so hot. After all she was on holiday. Why shouldn't she sleep? And she would wake up soon enough. Just as soon as the German divers arrived and they started dragging all their cases and dive bags along the inner ring road. And then she would go and find Gordo and they could get the drinks lined up in the bar to welcome the divers home.

'Wake up, Miranda.' Miranda stared dazed at Jim smiling down at her.

'Jim … I was calling for you. There was something on the path … no, it was in the mangroves … and I … Gordo wasn't there …'

The dream dissolved and Miranda sat up. The lights were on in the room and the curtains were drawn.

'Are you back from your dive?' she asked idiotically. And then, 'But what time is it?'

'Dinner time. That's why I woke you. The buffet opens in twenty minutes and I'm starving. If you want to have a shower, the bathroom's free.'

'I must have slept for hours.' She tried to gather herself together.

'Oh, you were out cold. I left you to it. I think you've just caught up on last night.'

'Yes. Except now I won't be able to sleep tonight either. The boat was back late, wasn't it? Did something happen?'

'No. Nothing. We had a great dive. No mantas yet. But some great sharks.'

'Not great white sharks!'

'Hardly. Not out here. Anyway, they are perfectly safe if properly dived. I've told you.' And indeed he had, as he, Mal and Gordo had made some appalling plan to go cage diving with the great whites in Oz somewhat later in the dive year.

33

'We were back right on time. I've already showered and changed once, and done a night dive with Patrick.'

'You're joking.'

'I told you, you were spark out. Hurry up and have that shower, I want to get to dinner. I'm starving.'

The bathroom was steamy hot, with fiery red oleander flaming through the roof, nodding to its glorious cousins in the bathroom flowerbed. The shower was Aussie-type, with an enormous shower head. It was like standing under a waterfall. And Miranda could look up and see the bright stars of the tropics.

'I can't believe I slept through all that – the luggage being dragged to the chalets this afternoon.'

She was drying herself quickly with one of the smallish sandpapery bath towels, watched by the Bathroom Cockroach, snug in his loo roll nest. So far he seemed to be holding to their compact. Apparently cockroaches did quite a good job of tidying up bathrooms from any little bits of nastiness lying about. And Miranda had read an even odder thing. That slugs were good at dealing with bathroom mould. They would simply graze over it as the parrot fish grazed on the algae on the reef, if there was anyone prepared to give them the chance. If only above water slugs were as beautiful as the underwater version, then it might almost be worth having them in your bathroom. They do come in designer colours, after all.

Insects were one of Miranda's many tropical island worries. She usually got bitten quite badly by invisible things that lived in the sand. Although the wretched little thorns seemed to have taken the job on this year, she thought, scratching crossly at her leg. Both the above and below water plant life seemed to have taken bites out of her.

Even Carmen Miranda might find it hard to deal with insects. Kicking such tiny backsides would require a lot more subtlety than poor Carmen was ever likely to possess. And she wouldn't be allowed to be scared of them, of course. She would have to get her own spiders out of the bath.

If only I could see the insects for what they are, Miranda thought. The most perfectly designed little mechanical toys. Because aren't they really the robot servants that scientists keep trying to invent? They must have been made to come out at night to clean up crumbs off the carpet. Or to clean the fallen leaves off the paths, and save the island men a job. Or to graze, sluggishly, over the algae on our bathroom tiles. And how the pavements of England could do with an influx of giant dung beetles!

Yet the insects were more than robots. Miranda had seen, on one of the nature programmes she and Jim watched together, a small mother beetle turn and defend her brood of miniscule toddlers from a monstrous praying thing that was looming up over the leaf they were trekking across. The tiny mother had fought valiantly, with Miranda cheering and begging the camera crew to intervene, and she had saved all but one of her tiny brood from a monster more horrid than anything that ever came out of one of Hollywood's giant cornflake packets. The little mother had shown that love and courage had been built into her by her Maker. Could Science match that?

But why were insects so panic-inducing? And how had they got so dangerous that they necessitated the invention of chemicals as life-threatening as they apparently were?

It seemed to Miranda there must be some disorder in the world, some dysfunction. Could it be that there was once an order to things, but they got disordered. But that sent her right back to the first chapters of Genesis. And few people nowadays would thank you for harking back to Genesis.

Miranda set about refining her theory that there was in fact only one plot in the world. Things got disordered and had to be put right again. It could be that murder had disturbed the order, and the murderer had to be found and punished. It could be that two people in love had some obstacles in the way of their organizing themselves neatly as a couple. And those obstacles had to be removed. And by coming to these islands, didn't they cause disorder?

'Will you get a move on!'

Miranda stopped daydreaming and got back to the business of getting herself dry. Which was a very temporary condition in the tropics. She wielded the small sandpapery towel as fast as she could; hoping that there might be big fluffy bath sheets here the next time they came.

'I'm not surprised you didn't wake up though. Nobody came in this afternoon. Aargh!' In his wanderings in and out of the bathroom, Jim had spotted the cockroach and was about to swat it.

'Oh don't, Jim.' Miranda begged 'It's left us alone so far. Anyway, what do you mean nobody arrived? But what about those German divers, and Gordo?'

Jim glowered at the cockroach, lowering his current paperback. 'Well, you know there was a storm on the main island? It was really bad. Wolfie says the word is that no planes could land. I think the Germans are probably still at Frankfurt. And, even if their plane got in before the weather struck, nothing could come out here. Well, not as far as the outer atolls anyway. It's a good thing we are so far out, or we'd have missed the day's diving.'

'Ah, that's probably why there was such a swell on the reef.' Miranda moved *The World's Greatest Diving Disasters in Tropical Waters* back into the bedroom in the interests of cockroach safety. There was a lurid flock of sharks surrounding a worried looking diver on the front cover.

She remembered her morning fright. 'Jim, there was such a lot of water pouring over the reef top into the lagoon this morning that I did wonder … It's silly I suppose … but, well, sharks couldn't get into the lagoon could they? I mean big ones, not like those darling baby ones last year.'

'They weren't baby sharks,' Jim said, exasperated, 'I told you a million times they were mullet. Not sharks. I don't care how savagely they went for their breadcrumbs.'

36

They squabbled amicably about it during the fragrant evening walk to the dining hall, holding sticky hands under the tropical stars.

EVENING

The Shoal had the dining room to themselves once more. There didn't even seem to be that many staff, just their waiter, one of the many Mo's, and the benevolent guy who presided over the soup tureen. There was a full quota of helpers in the kitchen though, judging by the hot platters of steaks and fries and battered chicken, the table of chopped vegetables, the fresh reef fish, and the desserts, with their curly cream toppings. The Shoal ate and ate, but the whole gorgeous buffet looked untouched when they left for the bar, in spite of all their efforts.

'What happens to all the leftovers,' Miranda wondered out loud. 'I suppose the staff has them?' Inga, dazzling in a cream and gold silk sheath, sipped at her flowery cocktail and said that no, the staff had their own kitchens where they cooked the fiery curries of the region.

'That's what we had when we first used to come to the Islands.'

Jim had been twenty years younger then, thought Miranda sadly. They had never thought they could ever get old. She suddenly noticed that Inga and Samir, Wolfie's third in command, were holding hands. Inga and Samir! She had no idea.

'We had fish curries. If we could catch any fish that is.'

'Yes, and no chalets, just the dhonis. Or the palm trees to sleep under.' Mal joined in the nostalgic chorus.

'What about the loos?' worried Miranda, toilet facilities being a constant in her Top Ten Travel Worries list.

'We just nipped behind the nearest palm tree. Or, on the fancier islands there might be a hole in the ground. And two jars of water. One for washing your bum. One for washing your hands.'

'And you'd better not forget which was which.' Patrick arrived with Trish and a tray of drinks.

Miranda thought sadly of her own toilet sur l'herbe experiences. Every tree she had ever had to nip behind had concealed nettles, or the tropical equivalent. She wondered how Carmen Miranda, her tropical alter ego, managed such things. And when and where Inga and Samir had met before, given that Inga was such a new diver. They had hardly had time to get to hand-holding stage on Small Island. Or was she being hopelessly old-fashioned again? Aha, but didn't Inga go to the Club Med Island last year. And come back all keen to learn diving? Was that a clue or what, my dear Watson?

'When did you lot first meet Wolfie?' Alison suddenly asked. The Shoal had followed Wolfie from island to island, as he ran such excellent diving holidays, but nobody, least of all Jim, seemed to remember exactly where and when they had first got together.

Miranda wanted to ask Inga, 'When did you first meet Samir?' but thought she better hadn't. It was probably something she was supposed to know anyway. Everyone else seemed to.

'So what do we all think of Mrs Wolfie?'

'Wolfie is married?!' Miranda was amazed. He had been sought after and single the last time she had islanded with him. And what must it be like to be a married couple living and working on this tiny island? You would be jammed together with your partner and a few staff, and the management, none of whom seemed to have families on the island.

There was the elusive Al-Auddin and his entourage, of course. But he probably didn't socialize with the hired help, and certainly not with the likes of the Shoal. And there were the holidaymakers, coming and going. There wasn't really a slack season here. Even if the dive boats couldn't go out, there were always white sand beaches to lie on, sunshine to tan in, and the lagoon to play in. Miranda sipped at her Banana Manana, which was the Cocktail of the Day. She wondered if it shouldn't really be called the Cocktail of Tomorrow, and never be available today. And she thought about the girl who lived on Small Island all the time. 'So what's she like then? Is she going to be able to hack it here?'

'Jassie? Wor, she's a bit of alright, alright.' Jim spoke through a mouthful of beer.

The male half of the Shoal joined in the chorus of appreciation. Or rather Todd and Patrick did. Mal said nothing. He, apparently, had eyes only for Diane. Which was just as it should be. OK. So Mrs Wolfie was under 40. With a bust. But what do us ladies think, she wondered.

'She's really nice.' Good-natured Trish would have to be very pushed not to say that. 'Strong-minded though.'

'She'll need to be, to be married to Wolfie.' Alison also appeared surprised that he had got married, even suggesting that as he had his pick of the prettiest tourists every year, it would never last.

Wolfie was strikingly good looking, with his sunbleached hair, deep tan and vivid blue eyes. But he was quite reserved, and didn't come across as a Casanova. Alison had been out on previous trips on Wolfie's other islands. Could she and Wolfie …? She sounded a bit savage about him. Alison didn't seem to have much luck with men. Miranda thought that, in a way, she didn't help herself by always going round in a threesome with Inga and Diane. Inga was tall, blonde and tanned, and Diane tiny and vivid, with her spiky black hair, green eyes and diamond cut features. And rings at every corner. Alison, with her medium height, medium brown hair, medium brown eyes, seemed to fade away between them. The eye was always drawn from Inga to Diane and back again, and Alison didn't get noticed.

Why do I never know what's going on, Miranda thought worriedly. Look how Inga and Samir got past me. There is plenty of novelist's material just within this group. Think of the Diane, Gil and Mel situation. Which is so unresolved. Or the Pats: Patrick and Patricia, are they really a golden couple? After all, they have a divorce or two behind them. Yet somehow, worried Miranda, I can't see what the story is. And anyway don't you have to be very perceptive about people to write a novel? Full of all this feminine intuition I am supposed to have?

And what did Miranda know about the world of single girls? Miranda had met Jim when she was seventeen, and married him at eighteen. As for the world of single expat girls in the twenty first century. It was a mystery, and she didn't think she would ever catch up with it. Well, to the matters in hand. She must go down to the boat early tomorrow morning. And say Hi to Wolfie, and meet his wife. Jassie. That's a pretty name. And she was bound to be pretty if she was Wolfie's wife. And nice too?

Never use the word 'nice' Miranda! Where did that surface from? And anyway, shouldn't it be: From where did that surface? Miranda felt that tiredness and tropical heat were making her incoherent. She needed her bed. And she just hoped that she would sleep the night through with no more of those vivid, uneasy tropical dreams.

THE SECOND DAY

'Its Gordo, at the door!' Miranda was jerked upright by the urgent knocking, and found herself in their quiet chalet bedroom, Jim fast asleep beside her.

Whatever woke her up? A pattering, a clattering on the roof? Her watch said 1.15. How annoying. She might as well trek off to the bathroom now she was awake.

The shrubs growing under the open bathroom roof were wet, and the spare toilet roll was soggy. It had been monsooning out there while they slept. Perhaps it was the last flurry of the rain that woke her, thought Miranda. She opened the front door a crack and looked out. Water was running everywhere, dripping from the trees, pouring off the roof. The Bathroom Cockroach was probably out there somewhere, hiding under a leaf, until it was safe to fly back to his flooded home. The waves were fierce against the island edge. Miranda felt she must just slip out and have a look at the tumbled night ocean.

Obviously, beyond the island, the storm was still raging. If Gordo and the next boat of divers didn't make it sometime in the next twenty four hours, it would hardly be worth coming. They were only here for a week. What a shame if they were going to miss all this! Miranda watched the huge waves riding over the reef and swallowing up the beach. The air was full of perfume. Frangipani, and something else – sandalwood perhaps? And so strong it was as if someone somewhere was burning a whole sandalwood log.

Miranda turned to look inland, almost expecting to see smoke rising from large incense holders somewhere. Maybe something exotic was going on behind the mysterious walls of the Aladdin palace. But the island was quiet and dark, the edge of the storm rustling gently at the tree tops. She could walk round the beach tonight. The sand had stayed home in spite of the fierce waves and ringed the island with a halo of white, glistening in the moonlight. She would feel more settled when Gordo arrived. He was the perfect dive buddy for Jim. He would be safe then. And the Shoal would be complete. Which wasn't at all what Miranda had meant to think. Jim was a very safe diver, as were all taught by him. She needed to walk. And then sleep. And not dream.

Miranda's dreams in the tropics were always vivid and disturbing; but only fragments of them caught and held as she woke up. She could remember nothing of the dream that had woken her this time, beyond Gordo trying to say something or do something. Had he been warning her about something? She must go … or she must not go … She felt she was glad not to remember it.

The rain had stopped, but drops still fell from the leaves in a steady drizzle. So what if I get wet, she thought. I'll be dry again in a few minutes. She would go right round the island, double quick time. Exercise would help. But she had hardly gone two steps from the chalet when she was stopped by the sound of quiet sobbing. Someone was among the trees, as hidden as they could be. Crying. And it was Trish.

Miranda tiptoed back to the villa. Quickly stifling a shriek as another of the horrible thorn plants ambushed her on the path. It was clear that the last thing Trish – sunny, sociable Trish – wanted at the moment was any kind of company.

Trish. Crying. Out on her own under the palm trees. At this time of night! In the middle of a monsoon!! Why? All she did know for sure, was that Trish didn't want anyone to see her, or to know about it.

But Trish and Patrick were the ideal couple. Miranda had thought they were always as sunny as a tropical island. She thought they had left their problems behind when they found each other. Suddenly she felt terribly tired, and rather depressed. She would give up her walk and go back to bed, although she would never be able to sleep now. Trish crying, on a Jim holiday.

Quietly, Miranda tucked herself back in, next to the sleeping Jim. He looked tranquil and boyish. If only she could join him in the world of sleep. But Trish was crying out there, so close. And so hidden – with such stifled sobbing. Did she want ...? Didn't she want ...? Should Miranda ...? Shouldn't she ...? While Miranda argued with her various selves about what she should do, sleep overtook her as softly as the tides swallowed up the white sand outside their door.

And soon Gordo took her hand. Together they walked in the velvet night to dive into another chalet, another world. They watched from the wall, alongside the Bathroom Cockroach, as Patrick and Trish showered together in silence.

How quickly that would change thought Miranda, if they knew we were here. And, yes, she had got that right. Because look at that thought bubble above Trish's head: 'How different he would be if one of the group knocked at the door. There'd be no Icy Silence then! It'd be non-stop jokes. The Party Patrick hat would go on in an instant.'

But they did know they had an audience. Why else would they be showering with their clothes on?

'It'd be all bonhomie then. It's almost psycho the way he can change at the drop of a hat.'

So that is the colour of sadness. The colour underneath Trish's golden tan.

Patrick, having strewn his damp towels all over the room, was sorting out his dive gear quickly and efficiently. Various bubbles floated above his head: 'She'll be all smiles the minute we join up with the group.' 'It's us. It's what we do. The life and soul of the party pair.' 'We do it so well together.' 'It's all good between us. Apart from ...'

The bubble blurred, and Miranda couldn't read it. But the others were clear enough. 'Typical woman. She can't just be happy with all we have. She wants everything. And she'll spoil what we have for that.' 'If she did have everything, she'd throw that away too!' 'Just like her mother, Eve.'

He glanced at her as she silently restored order to their room. 'She is so lovely. Not young anymore. But I've had it with young girls after Kelly. Had it.'

Trish's profile was beautifully carved. Her dark brown lashes curling and framing startled brown eyes. Her skin was always tanned to an even brown. Her hair, still glossy brown, had a natural curl to it, so that it would spring back into shape after the stormiest of boat rides. 'Tall and slender, long, long legs. She is everything I want. Everything. I have it all.' 'Why won't she just be content with that?'

Now their bubbles began to converge. 'He has got what he wants, why can't he see that I don't have everything I want?' 'And at least admit that it's not alright, that I am missing something.' 'If he would only acknowledge that we can't both have what we want, and I am the one who is missing out.' 'Why does he blame me for what happened before?'

Anger, hurt, bitterness. But, underneath, there was something else, something that could grow, if they would let it. Something good, and potentially strong. Something full of hope. Miranda thought it was love, real love.

'Gordo.' Miranda saw her thought bubble float past. 'You are a great dream buddy.'

A large clear bubble floated from the Bathroom Cockroach. It was hard to translate. It either said, 'Flaky bits of fallen skin, yummy, yummy,' or something much more profound.

Miranda launched another bubble. 'I didn't know you ate out,' it seemed to say.

Oh Yuk.

She woke up, cross. 3.15! What was it about the tropics? Why could she never sleep the night through these days? She might as well go to the bathroom now she was awake, but she decided not to look to see if her cockroachy friend was there. After all she had just met him in her dreams. She didn't really want to meet him in her bathroom too.

But surely she hadn't really been dreaming about the cockroach? She could remember Gordo. Or was it Patrick? But the dreams evaporated as she tried to recall them, leaving only a tantalizing fragment. She had been standing outside Todd's villa, just about to rattle at his door to ask if Gordo could come out to play. But the Bathroom Cockroach had opened it before she could knock and silently shook its head.

'Children.'

'Children?' Miranda looked at Jim surprised. He had been fixing up his cameras when she told him about the crying in the night. He had said, 'Yes' and 'Uh-huh' a lot which had made her assume that she wasn't talking to him so much as thinking out loud.

But he had been listening, after all. 'That's the problem with Pat and Trish. Children. She wants them. He doesn't. He's done all that. And the old biological clock is ticking.'

'But, Jim, they would have sorted that out before they got married. Trish always knew about his children. She's had them to stay often enough.'

'Yes.' Jim clicked his largest camera and smiled confidently. There would be no repeat of the time he saw the whale shark and the camera let him down.

'But she thought she could change his mind once they were married. Bet you anything you like.' He sounded rather smug.

Miranda thought about it, and knew he was right. It was as if Jim had been reminding her of something that she already knew, but had forgotten. It explained quite a few odd little scenes and remarks. And an

47

indefinable tension in the air when Patrick's son and daughter were visiting. Something different from the usual step-parent tensions.

But how irritating, she thought. Why does Jim know what's going on? Aren't I supposed to be the one with intuition, who knows all and sees all, and smiles wisely at the follies and foolishness of men? Or have I been watching too many TV comedies?

'After all, he's got a son and a daughter.' Jim lugged the last of the dive baggage to the door. 'And he's just got them both through college. Why would he want to start again? Would we?'

They agreed they wouldn't, and talked about Emily all the way to the breakfast buffet. They couldn't decide whether she and Tim would be in Indonesia or Bali by now. But they had given up worrying. It was a typical Emily enterprise anyway, there was nothing reckless about it, and the London flat, rented out profitably while they were away, continued to pay its mortgage and increase in value by leaps and bounds. She hadn't left them too much to worry about.

Miranda noticed that Patrick and Trish walked to breakfast in a wounded silence, but holding hands. Mal and Diane, equally silent, walked ahead of them – and they weren't holding hands. Inga and Alison looked happy though, having a pleasurable walk to breakfast, turning the Mal, Gil, Diane situation inside out, and giving it a good airing. Flowers and frangipani scent could not compete and passed by them unregistered. They talked intensely and quietly through breakfast, drawing a little apart from the others, leaving most of the enormous plateful of food they had collected from the buffet uneaten. Miranda hoped that she and Jim were too boring to be the subject of much discussion.

She planned to do quite a lot of watching, and note-taking and dialogue collecting, as this was her big day. This was the day she went out on the dive boat, with the Shoal. It was just to be a morning dive. Not too far off. They would be back for lunch, before the worst of the sun.

Being on the boat gave a refreshing spring clean to her worries list. Many things simply had to disappear, or shrink way back down the top hundred, to make room for all the new ones. Storms would be the number one legitimate worry, as their local one was still monsooning away over the horizons of the small island, cutting them off from any new visitors. Just suppose the weather suddenly blew up here? And then there was the question of the seaworthiness of the boat – although Mo and Wolfie were known to run a very tight operation.

But boats did go down. There was no question about that. And suppose, for instance, they met a school of ravenous killer whales. Or that a tanker towing a skyscraper to New York caught fire, just as a comet on a previously safe orbit around …

'We don't often see you on the boat, Miranda.' Jim and Wolfie had obviously finished their briefing as Mal was now talking to her.

'Nope.' Miranda had long ago found that it was better never to explain or complain about diving matters. But she was hoping the general dive chatter would start. Trish and Patrick were quiet for once, both lost in their books, or their thoughts. As was Jim, now he had got everything sorted out. She couldn't see what he was reading, but it would almost certainly be the Cockroach Squasher. Or had he started on *Dive Boat Disasters – A Compendium of Current Calamities*?

Mal and Diane were quiet too. Todd was up front with Wolfie and they were talking animatedly about something but Miranda couldn't hear them above the sound of the boat and the waves. However Todd was probably discussing his optimistic theory that the whole of Air Scandinavia's stewardess crew were going to turn up on Small Island any moment now. Perhaps that is how Carmen could sneak herself on to the island, hiding in the midst of a clutch of tall tanned blondes?

Inga and Alison were down the other end, with their cameras, trying to get the optimum shot of a disappearing Small Island. But the spray was proving a problem. They were a small Shoal this year. Sometimes there were as many as thirty. Still, a small shoal for a small island seemed right. Surely it would sink back into the ocean if too many visitors loaded with luxurious expectations landed on it.

'So, Mal, what are you hoping to see today?' Miranda realized she hadn't listened to a word of Jim and Wolfie's briefing, which was annoying as it might have proved very useful for *Carmen – The Return!!*, or some future tome. But it was exhilarating, flying through the ocean like this.

'The eel reef. The currents are just right this morning, so we should see great coral and morays.'

Ah. This would be a good dive for Jim, then. His coral garden shots were among his best sellers, and today he could get some more. He'd be down there stroking eels too. There were already some good shock horror prints of Jim stroking morays, his ungloved hand very close to the big white teeth – teeth so big and white that they almost rivalled Carmen's Hollywood gnashers.

And where was the wretched woman? She was supposed to be with Miranda, inspiring her to produce her blockbuster – distracting her from worries if only by producing strange new things to worry about. Miranda hoped she wasn't lurking down there somewhere, waiting for some foolish diver to try to stroke her.

'Nothing too big today then, Mal? And lots of macro shots?' Miranda pulled herself politely back to the conversation.

'You never know in this ocean. You could see anything – any size. Or so everyone tells me. We could see rays or sharks, as I understand it.'

'No. Not sharks. I'm not even sure I want to be in the water with rays. They are so big.' That was Diane. And Alison chimed in with, 'The macro stuff will do for me. Those darling little clowns.'

'Hi.' Todd joined in suddenly. 'Those little guys are savage. They'll attack anything whatever the size.'

'Well, they feel so safe with their anemones.' Miranda hoped some foolish clownfish wouldn't take it into his head to annoy Todd while there wasn't an anemone for it to run back to.

'You mean those gorgeous anemones are poisonous too! Is there anything in this sea that isn't poisonous?' The boat was suddenly too small, as divers struggled to get inside wet suits, or BCD's. There was much clearing and cleaning of masks.

The sea was as it was – blue green and wavy. Miranda wondered what signal had set them off. If she put on diving goggles and a pair of flippers would she see a large sign with an arrow pointing downwards and the words, 'You have reached the Reef,' emblazoned on it? Well, it was to find out all these things that she had come along. And to glean some dialogue. Which she hadn't so far. In fact she would have to remember to discard some dialogue. The words 'goggles and flippers' should never ever be heard on a dive boat. They were 'masks and fins' and don't you forget it!

They weren't very far from Small Island. She could still see it, dotting the horizon. This reef could actually be an outcropping of the island itself. The islands were the tips and tops of underwater mountain chains, after all. This reef could be like the South Ridge of Everest, perhaps, leading down to a lesser peak? A peak that, in time, would be born as Small Small Island. A younger brother or sister.

She occasionally still wondered if they should have provided a sibling for Emily. But, somehow, it hadn't happened. And Emily didn't seem to feel any lack. She and Jim were both only children, and perhaps hadn't really thought enough about establishing any other kind of family.

She was glad that they were going to dive within sight of Small Island. Maybe there was a chance of the storm hitting, and that was why Mo and Wolfie had brought them here. They could run for home at any time and be quickly back in the safe embrace of Small Island. That would be logical.

And to be embraced by Small Island was to be safe? Of course. Nowhere could be more friendly. Apart from those thorns. Miranda scratched irritably at her leg. How sensible the divers were in their nylon skins. She almost felt she would have to borrow one for her walks round the island.

Now the Shoalers were disappearing one by one over the side. Samir and Wolfie had taken Alison and Diane down. Mal was keen that Diane get confident under the big water, as he had loads of wet holidays lined up for them. He wanted them to go kelp diving in California and Florida where the sea-cows lived. And up to the Barrier Reef to swim with the giant cod – as big as buses. Potato Cod they were called. Which was funny, albeit in bad taste, given the fish and chip connection.

Would anyone be so ruthless and unkind as to hijack the trusting fish for such purposes? Hopefully not. Anyway, Miranda seemed to remember that Jim had said they weren't that sort of cod. Where was Jim, anyway? Who was he diving with? And what a shame Gordo hadn't got here yet. This was a reef full of photo ops. Ah. He was with Mal. And Todd and Inga made an interesting pair. What was that expression as he looked at her? 'In your dreams, Todd,' Carmen would say if she happened by.

Inga was now changing from the briefest of white shorts and top into hot pink and black dive accessories. She disappeared over the side in a dazzling way, almost worthy of Carmen herself. Not that anyone could look completely glamorous once they had that regulator thing in their mouth. In fact, Carmen Miranda probably wouldn't dive. Those teeth could not be dimmed by scuba equipment. Miranda lay back, careful to keep all bits of herself in the shadow of the awning, and looked at her notebook. Her head seemed to be empty of ideas – and full up with worries. This holiday wasn't being nearly as relaxing as usual.

Was everyone having a good time? That was always the big worry about a group, especially as Jim simply refused to worry about it. I've organized a wonderful dive holiday. If they can't enjoy it, that's their fault. Miranda scolded herself in Jim's voice. Here she was on an empty dive boat. Well, OK, it wasn't empty. Two of the Mo's were still aboard. Mo the driver – the older Mo, and Mo the … younger. So, alright, the boat probably wasn't going to drift away into the deep ocean, leaving Miranda and the Mo's to die of thirst, and the divers to return to find no boat, and to drown on the surface.

But suppose … the conquering tropical sun prevailed over the Miranda worry list, and the next thing she knew she was under the blue green water, with Gordo. Jim had said she must take him to them as soon as he arrived. His train had pulled in, with all his luggage, and they had stepped off the platform into the water. But which way was it to Shark Point? Why had they gone to Shark Point anyway? That was so dangerous. And where you had sharks, you had currents. She and Gordo would be pulled away before they could find the boat … and already something had got hold of her legs. It was biting her. And burning.

Help me, Gordo!

But Gordo wasn't there after all, she had made some kind of mistake. They had all gone to Eel Reef, with Gordo. She had come here alone. Alone to a hot and deadly danger, deep under the deceptive cream frills of the seething ocean.

Miranda woke to find the sun had moved around and her legs were reddening. It was especially painful on all her bites. Her shawl. She scrabbled round in her bag and found the large silk shawl she had bought some years ago on Another Island, and wrapped it well around herself and moved back into the shade. But now she couldn't sleep. The water seemed calmer and bluer. The turquoise had faded. She leant over the side looking into the depths, hoping to see a Shoaler coming up to the surface. She wanted a signal that the dive would soon end.

There were no divers, but plenty of rainbow fish, sparkling around the boat. So entrancing – painted by a master craftsman. If I was a designer, thought Miranda, I would come here for inspiration. It's almost as if there really was a master Designer, a Painter … a Creator … Miranda gasped, and jumped back. For a moment she almost thought that she had gone and conjured up the ghastly Carmen, with her white teeth. But it was only a flying fish, jumping right at her face out of the water. You foolish thing. Suppose I had been a predator. You would have flown straight into my mouth, Miranda scolded as it flapped back into the sea.

But she was a predator though, wasn't she? What would she be having for lunch if not the island fish? Why? Why was everything so cruel, when it ought to be perfect? Why wasn't there an array of beautiful, tasty seaweeds to eat? And sea-mushrooms? If you could have sea-slugs, then why not sea-mushrooms? There were such things as sea-cucumbers, but Miranda felt sure they too were a kind of fish. Were there sea radishes, and sea cress? And sea beetroot? She sighed, thinking of Yorkshire high teas of long ago, and looked over to where Mo and Mo sprawled under the awnings. They were deeply asleep, perfectly relaxed. Water or land, it was all the same to the island men.

Suppose Carmen was here, instead of Miranda? Would there be a flashy speedboat hurtling across the waves? It could either contain a conventionally handsome, dark-haired man bringing her chocolates, or a load of villains set on kidnapping her. It would depend on the state of her career at the time.

Miranda looked out across the water. No kidnappers or bringers of chocolates were bothering to speed her way. The waves seemed bigger though. Come on, Miranda, this is really a very glamorous bit of ocean. Don't tell me Carmen wouldn't be getting up to something. Perhaps she'd be rising through the waves, a gleaming knife in her dazzling teeth. A load of sharks would be muttering jealously in her wake, rubbing their sore bottoms, and carping about what they could have achieved, toothwise, with a bit of Hollywood dentistry. But what would she be rising up through the waves for? Miranda really couldn't think of anything for the tiresome woman to do. She could be facing the deranged crew, clad only in a white thong – Carmen Miranda, not the crew, of course. Miranda sighed, and looked over to where the crew slumbered on. There was nothing interesting enough to keep them awake. Face it, Miranda. And go back to sleep yourself. But she couldn't.

Back to the fish then, as both Carmen and sleep had completely failed her. There were parrot fish around the boat. They were the signature fish of the islands. They flaunted their impossible beauty even off the utilitarian jetty just outside the airport where the boats set off for the various islands. What must it be like to be as lovely as that? And why weren't we all? Miranda leant right over the boat, watching as the parrot fish glided gracefully into the blue deep. How to describe its beauty in words? For instance, how could she describe the quality of whiteness of that fish just approaching the boat ...?

Miranda jumped. It was white alright. But a face. Not a fish. Inga's face. But her tan seemed to have been washed off somehow. And that was Jim and Jassie. Holding her in the water. Struggling with her. Inga's eyes were closed. Dark lashes on white cheeks. She looked as if she would sleep for ever. But Jim wouldn't let her. He was kissing her awake. Where was Todd? Wasn't he the one who wanted to do that?

Her eyelids were fluttering. Or was it just that a wave was breaking over the strugglers, rippling hair and eyelashes. Another wave crashed over them. More struggles broke out. Miranda looked round for something to reach them with. Something to pull them in.

But Elder Mo was already over the side with the inflatable rings, and Young Mo was reaching forward with the boathook. Jim was shouting something. Then kissing Inga again. Jassie was now at the boat. She held out her hand. Which unfroze Miranda, who reached out to help her on board.

Who could have believed that bronzed Inga could look so pale? Shock. She was in shock. Jassie had dispatched Young Mo underwater with a blackboard message, and was talking urgently with Elder Mo. 'Return to Boat IMMEDIATELY!!' the blackboard said. How would it feel to see those words coming at you underwater? It was going to wipe the suntan off the rest of the Shoal's faces. Miranda expected a lot of pale Shoalers to come bobbing up any minute now. She only hoped the shock of the notice wasn't going to cause any more problems. But for the moment she was occupied with Jim's barked commands about wrapping Inga up. She had found a few towels and did her best, but Inga was shivering. Shivering in the tropical heat. Her hands were like marble. Samir appeared. He held her tenderly.

Inga and Samir. They had been sitting close together in the bar of an evening, talking, talking. No wonder she had been looking so dreamy. This was really serious.

Really serious. Miranda shook herself back to reality and found more towels. And tried to warm Inga up. Jim was called to the side. Someone was trying to get back on the boat. She could hear the voices. Worried, urgent. Someone called Samir for help. So Miranda wadded up her scarf under Inga's head and Inga sank back. She was trying to say something. Miranda craned forward to hear. Something about pulled me down. It pulled me down? He pulled it down?

Miranda's heart jumped sickeningly in her chest. She hadn't said, '*She pulled me down*,' had she? This terrible new creation couldn't somehow have escaped from her head and got loose among the divers? Miranda told herself to calm down and stay rational. And keep talking calmly and reassuringly to Inga, as she seemed to be doing.

Anyway, there would be no point at all in Carmen getting out of her head and going on the rampage. Stephen King had already covered that territory. That film had already been made. What was the woman playing at?

Elder Mo seemed to be trying to start the boat. But were all the divers aboard? Miranda looked round. Diane and Alison were turning out their bags, on a search for dry towels to warm the shivering Inga. Jassie was organizing Mo the Boathook. Pat and Trish were getting out the whisky. And bringing it over.

'Inga,' said Trish softly. 'Have a sip of this. It's going to warm you up.' Inga sat up weakly, sipped, shuddered and closed her eyes again.

'We need more towels, woollies, anything you have,' Miranda appealed to them.

Trish went off to rummage through their dive bags.

'What happened to her?'

'I don't know, Patrick. She says someone pulled her down.' Miranda felt another strange pang of guilt.

They'll have to treat me for shock if I start raving on about Carmen and her teeth, and one patient is enough, Miranda told herself firmly. Anyway, Mal the Dentist was on board just in case the Terrible Teeth had got out of control. Miranda knew that she mustn't start laughing, because if she did, she wouldn't be able to stop.

'It's OK, Miranda, Jim and Todd will be back up in a few minutes. And Inga's going to be OK. I think she must have just got a bit deep or something.' Mal must have seen the shock on her face.

'Yes, she got pulled down.' It pulled her down. It. That was surely what she said.

Inga closed her eyes weakly. Tears ran down her pale face.

'Just give her a bit of space. She's in shock.' That was Jassie, taking charge. She put her arms round Inga, to comfort and warm her. Miranda's heart gave an even greater leap. Mal had said Jim and Todd would be up in a few minutes. Jim must have gone back down there. He wasn't on the boat. They mustn't go without him.

'Where's Jim! I don't see him.'

'It's OK, Miranda.' Mal put his arm round her shoulder reassuringly. 'He's gone back down to take Todd a spare air. He grabbed her you know, Todd did. She suddenly went down, like she was on a lift, and Todd managed to shoot after her and grab her regulator. Unfortunately, he pulled it out of her mouth. But he got her.'

Miranda looked blankly at him. None of it made any sense. And what about Jim?

'Jim made sure Todd stopped. That's why he and Jassie brought Inga up. They got her breathing again on the surface. Jim went straight back down to be with Todd. He seemed alright, but who knows. Jim took a pony bottle just to be sure. He must do a really good safety stop.'

Ah. The jigsaw of pieces in Miranda's head began to click into place. Safety stop – of course. You didn't shoot straight up to the surface when you had been diving. You had to come up slowly to make sure the nitrogen left your body. Unless, of course, you had stopped breathing. Then they rushed you to the surface no matter what. And the nitrogen inside you began to bubble. And then you got bent. But Miranda also knew the rule that Jim hammered into his divers. You must never, never hold your breath when you come up. Or you will burst your lungs. She turned to look at Inga. She was pale. And cold. And shocked. But definitely breathing. Thank God. Thank God.

'It's bad enough having one casualty. We don't want two.'

'How deep did Todd go?' That was Patrick, asking for all the divers.

'Don't know. We'll have to see what his computer says.'

'But …' Diane was bewildered. 'Where did Inga sink down to? We were on the bottom anyway.'

'No,' Mal corrected her. 'That was only a platform between reefs. It suddenly sloped away to the deep ocean. She was just over the slope, taking a picture of that feather star.'

'Oh yes, it was lovely. It had walked out to the end of the whip coral. We took it too. Or I did.' Trish suddenly went a bit pale, probably thinking that there, but for the grace of God, went any one of them. Alison and Diane looked at each other. Miranda had a feeling that the dive boat had seen the last of them. They hadn't liked the ocean currents from the start, and this would have confirmed all their worst fears.

DECOMPRESSION

The decompression chamber turned out to be opposite the palace of Al-Auddin. It was hidden by a wall of oleander and bamboo, the tiny signpost buried in the florid growth of the tropics. There was a resident doctor and nurse. Or usually there was. Unfortunately, as Wolfie had explained, they were both currently stranded off-island by the storm. However, Jassie was well qualified, and she didn't think Inga seriously bent – thanks to Todd's prompt actions. But she would need to stay in the chamber for a while.

Miranda followed Wolfie, Jassie, Inga, Jim and a frantic Samir. Another of those wretched thorn bushes ambushed her bare ankles. Jassie unlocked the door of the tiny clinic, which was so well hidden by thorns and mangroves and fragrant tropical flowers, that no diver would even have to think about it in passing. Now Inga would be restored. She would be locked away in the chamber until she was herself again, unbent, straightened out. Safe.

They set off towards the bar, for a reviving beer – all except Samir, who opted to stay and watch over Inga until morning. Jassie would pop in at regular intervals until there was a doctor to take over. These tropical storms didn't usually last too long, and this one had already outstayed its welcome. Poor Inga had looked very depressed, locked up in her pod. But she seemed to be getting over the shock. The colour had returned to her face. There was a bit of a hysterical edge to her, but that was understandable. Apparently, the feather star had been walking in a tantalizing way back from the end of its whip coral, beautifully silhouetted against the clear water of the ocean below, and she had swum off reef a bit to position herself, when, suddenly, a current got her.

'It felt exactly as if someone had grabbed hold of my feet,' she said. 'So scary. It was like a horror film.' And the next thing she could remember was being given whisky on the boat.

'I really hate whisky too,' said Inga mournfully. They had provided her with a flask of strong coffee in her chamber, and Miranda had brought all her magazines and newspapers from the flight. Anyway, they agreed, on their way back to the bar, she was OK. It had turned out alright in the end. Inga would have to spend a few hours a day in the chamber, just to be safe. There would be no more diving for her this holiday. It was even a good thing, they agreed, given it had to happen, that it had happened this end of the week. She should have no trouble flying home when the time came. If any of them could get home that is. After all, as long as the storm raged, no boats or planes could come out here to get them.

They then agreed that the island had done them well. Whatever was happening on the bigger islands, here at Small Island, the days had been sunny, and the dive boats had been able to go out. Not being too interested in the dive conversation, Miranda turned back to look at the palace and the surgery opposite. She could see bits of curly roof and a fairy-tale spire above the high, thorny wall of the Al-Auddin compound, but the surgery was swallowed up by the tropical green of Small Island as if it had never been there. Then an enormous cloud swam across the sun, and they all scuttled off to the bar before the giant raindrops of the tropics began to fall.

The sunset bar crowd were subdued that night. Inga's incarceration in the decompression chamber had quietened them. They needed her glamorous presence to get over it. Yet the feeling of relief was still in the air.

'Well, it could have been so much worse. I reckon she's going to be fine.' Trish looked on the bright side.

'I want to find out exactly what happened.' That was Jim, with Mal seconding.

'Todd, how are you? You really are a hero, you know!' They all chimed in with Trish to welcome Inga's rescuer, and Jim got up to get him a large whisky, or whatever he wanted. Todd was surprisingly modest and understated as a hero, and shrugged off Trish's compliments. The force of the rain outside kept them well in to the centre tables, as the lacy bamboo walls were open to the elements. It seemed there was a series of storms, traveling round the archipelago and refusing to leave. It happened some years, according to Wolfie, although this was much worse than usual.

There was not much let-up on Small Island that evening. It became as cold as a tropical island could get, till they were almost shivering in their skimpy tops and miniscule shorts. When Todd wasn't grumbling about that, he was grumbling about the food. They always had steak on the other island. Always. Fish wasn't human food as far as he was concerned. And as for green stuff! For once Miranda didn't let his mutterings get to her. Todd had come up trumps when it mattered.

They had talked the accident to death, during pre-dinner drinks, over dinner, and now had nothing more to say about it. It turned out that Inga had got caught in a strange current, like a whirlpool. Wolfie said he had never come across such a thing before, and intensive investigation with the island men produced the same result. They too had never heard of such a thing. Although they hadn't seemed to want to discuss it. The weather was strange all over the world though, and El Nino could be to blame as usual. After all, El Nino was a strange change in the ocean currents, wasn't it?

Still, whatever had grabbed Inga, she would have vanished into the deep ocean if Todd hadn't hurtled straight after her. Miranda wondered why he wasn't in decompression with her. She didn't like to ask, as the subject seemed to have been dropped by a silent, but general, consensus. Todd had done alright. Been a good dive buddy when the chips were down.

A character looking rather like Todd suddenly appeared in Miranda's mind. Al Nino. She could call him Al Nino. Should he be a glamorous baddy, as played by the young Al Pacino? And would he be a fit consort for Carmen? Was that him down there, grabbing away at any blonde that came to hand? Miranda gathered that, up until the accident, it had been a great dive. But nobody felt it was quite right to talk about that, so their chatter had returned to the food – the lack of the variety they had come to expect from the islands, even one as remote as this. It still seemed lavish to Miranda though, just with no steak that evening. Mal weighed in on the coconut front. Apparently, according to current dietary thinking, coconuts were bad for you. Stuffed full of cholesterol. You might as well go out and eat a dozen egg yolks as eat a coconut. Miranda didn't agree. It seemed obvious to her that God had made coconuts for us to eat. And given that the islanders didn't farm coconuts, and cram them into tiny cages, or pump them full of antibiotics and feed them on coconuts that had died of terrible diseases, then they must still be as their Creator made them. So how could they be bad?

There were no middlemen here to dictate an intensive farming policy. You simply shopped at the coconut palm, and it gave freely and generously. Miranda intended to go on eating them. Their white flesh was soft and blancmangey, not tough and stringy like the English version. Perhaps it was the stress of the long journey to Europe that packed the poor things full of cholesterol.

'At least the showers are still working.' She did a bit of Pollyanna-ing instead. 'A water shortage really would be a problem.'

'Yes, but we are on to stuff from the de-salination plant now.' That was Jassie. She and Wolfie and Elder Mo had come to join them, feeling the need of company after the shocks of the day. 'It's murder on the skin,' she said, patting her silky honey coloured cheek.

Where was this plant, Miranda wondered. She hadn't noticed anything resembling an industrial plant on Small Island. Probably it was as neatly hidden away as the decompression chamber.

'Just as long as we don't run out of beer.' Patrick, of course, but all the guys clutched their glasses nervously and Jim hurried off to the bar to get some more pints in while he could. Which gave the ladies of the party a chance to make a lot of merry remarks about the boys and their beer that kept everybody happy for a while.

Miranda thought how beautiful the island was at night. It glowed in the dark. There was phosphorescence on the invisible wave tops, phosphorescence on the leaping fish. And moonlit frangipani blossom, bruised by the rain, would still fill the air with sweetness once the storm stopped. It was such a tender little island. Miranda felt sorry for it, being battered by the enormous raindrops and having them clumping all over it with their great expat feet.

'So why is it called Small Island then, Patrick? Not just because it's so small?' She suddenly remembered the unfinished conversation of … was it only yesterday? The world outside the island was fading fast.

'Aha. Small Island.' Patrick held up his beer ceremoniously. 'It is called Small Island because …'

'Ah, come on Patrick, what would you know about what it's called.' Todd was already ahead of them in the drinking stakes.

But not because he's worried about Inga, thought Miranda. He's nervous about something. Not nervous, but … she couldn't find the word. Jumpy? Not exactly. And what good was she going to be with her novel if she couldn't find the words? He was not happy here. Not happy with this group, or this island or something. He was more of the Club Med type really. That was probably it.

'Oh, I know, Todd old lad. I know. I asked Mo.' That must be Mo the Waiter – the only waiter at the moment. 'I was wondering why there weren't many staff on the island and he told me that most preferred to leave the island at night – because … are you ready for this?'

The Shoal looked at him. Bored? Or Expectant? With mild polite interest in my case, thought Miranda, but I really can't speak for the others.

'Because something small comes ashore after dark.'

That caught Miranda's attention. It reminded her of something – something lost in her dreams somewhere. She repeated it, thoughtfully.

'Something small comes ashore after dark. That's what they think?'

'Yes, and that's why the name's so long you see. It really means something like the Island Where Something Small Comes Ashore After Dark.'

'And if it was the Island Where Something A Bit Larger Comes Ashore After Dark then I suppose it would take you your whole holiday week to pronounce.'

'We've already done that one, Mal!' Patrick leapt up to get the next round in. There was no queuing tonight, as the bar was empty apart from the Shoal – and Mo the Boathook, with his bartender's hat on.

'So it's a taboo island' Jim said thoughtfully.

'Oo-er. What does that mean?' Diane shuddered deliciously, while Alison looked … vacant … bored …?

'Well, someone didn't want people coming here, or at least, they didn't want them staying here overnight, so they made up this story to frighten them off. Apparently, the taboo is that it's fine during the day, but you must be gone before sunset.'

'But why?' Diane seemed fascinated.

'Well, there could be many reasons. For instance, perhaps someone was smuggling something, and kept the boats and everything here. Or perhaps there was an illicit still here.'

'An illicit what still here?' Diane asked, gormlessly.

'Still. Alcohol still. Poteen. Moonshine.'

'Or maybe the local bigwig kept a second harem here, and didn't want his first harem to find out about his night time visits.' That was Patrick, returning with a full tray of drinks.

'That's why the staff are off the island!'

'How do you mean?' They all turned to Trish, who seemed surprised they hadn't noticed how sparse the staff were this year.

'They don't stay on the island. Not the ones who live locally. They leave at night. They never have spent the night on this island. It simply isn't done. It's just the ones from the other atolls who sleep here. And sometimes they won't either.'

'Ah.' Jim had obviously been a bit puzzled. 'And of course they can't get back because of the monsoon.'

'Yup. That'll be it. I mean 'locally' must be quite a boat ride away.' Mal went on to complain that his room hadn't been cleaned and tidied when he got back from his dive.

'No, and it's not likely to be till this storm clears. We will just have to muck in and do our own.'

Todd launched into an expletive spattered diatribe at the very suggestion of doing his own housework. He would not do it at home, so why the hell should he do it on holiday?

'Hey, you can't legislate for storms.'

'Not yet, anyway.'

Thank goodness, thought Miranda. She was glad there were things they couldn't yet control. They had wrecked so much already. Including these islands, came the unwanted thought. But, she put up her usual defence, didn't the people want them here? Didn't they need them here? Tourists brought in hard currency. The rather handsome island currency, which included a large bronze coin, didn't make an appearance on the island – neither in the shops, nor on the bill. Everything was Yankee dollar price. And they could charge what they liked, thought Miranda, because these islands have everything us tourists want. Hot steamy beauty, and not too much crowding. No constant hassling to buy things, or to take taxis. There was no way a taxi driver could make a living on Small Island. You would get in the left hand door at Reception and get straight out through the right hand door to find your villa.

Something small? Well, at least whatever had caused the taboo in the first place, it wasn't any of Miranda's fault. There was nothing small about the shark-toothed heroine she had brought here. So they couldn't possibly have tabooed the place in anticipation of Carmen's visit. There was nothing sinister about the island anyway. In fact, tonight, there was something celebratory about it. It was full of joy.

Miranda left the Shoal at their drinks and wandered down to the jetty to watch the stars which shone so brightly above the waves, and the luminous fish as they leapt and danced in their night ballet. She was wondering what her uber-self would have felt about the bar session. Probably she would have been bored. She would require the sort of bar where handsome young waiters did acrobatic things with cocktail shakers.

But had Carmen's waiter almost dropped the shaker when Something Small was mentioned?

She decided to watch the sea instead. It was so much more beautiful than her would-be heroine. A shoal of slim dark somethings moved as one in the silvered water by the sleeping dive boat. She tried to cajole them with bread rolls from dinner, but they were not the fish of the day and, wary, they kept their distance. The wind got up, bouncing the waves on to the beach and causing coconuts to crash carelessly through the undergrowth. They were followed by Jim, with the remainder of his pint.

'Oh Jim, it's so lovely, I wish we could just stay out here all night.'

'You can,' said Jim the Practical, 'if you want to. Some of us happen to need a good night's sleep in a comfy bed as we're doing an early morning dive.'

'Who is going with you?' Miranda would rather none of them dived again on this trip but she knew that wasn't going to happen.

They moved away from the jetty and back towards the centre of the island. The moonlit beach was rapidly being swallowed up, leaving them no sand to walk on.

'Todd's going to come.'

'Todd! He'll never make it. He was drinking before happy hour and he was still in the bar when we left. What a shame Gordo hasn't got here yet.'

'If Todd says he'll be there, he'll be there. He likes the morning dives. It's a good hangover cure actually, an early morning plunge into warm water.'

Jim liked Todd, as he liked most people. And, once again, Miranda wished she could be more like him. She could see only too clearly how much pleasanter her life would be if she was. And she felt remorseful about her feelings re Todd. Somehow he frightened her. And made her feel inadequate, not really a woman at all. But if he hadn't risked going straight down after Inga … Miranda shuddered thinking of the fathomless ocean she saw when she had swum to the outer edge of the lagoon and looked over the coral wall.

'I wish I could like him though, Jim.'

'You don't have to like him. Or dislike him. I don't suppose he cares either way.'

Well, that was unarguable, and Miranda was about to put more of her Todd thoughts into words – they would be a soothing muzak to which Jim could mentally sort out his cameras for tomorrow – but she was distracted by their passing the magnificent gates of Al-Auddin's palace.

'Look! Jim, they've arrived. Well someone has. Someone's got here.'

They stepped gingerly up to the gates. There was a lot of thorn around them. It was beginning to wind its way up the closely worked lattice.

'Oh yes, there's a light in there. Lanterns. And music. So one boat got through anyway. I wonder if they are having a party. I don't see anyone yet. There must be another way in though, this door doesn't look as if it's used anymore.'

Jim was right. It was not only thorn-encrusted but also red with rust. Funny they hadn't noticed that the first time they looked. 'We must walk round it tomorrow and see where the real door is.'

THE THIRD DAY

'We should see mantas today. Wolfie says the fishermen saw them yesterday.' Jim had gathered his shrunken Shoal by the jetty for a pre-embarkation briefing.

Miranda wondered if she had heard that right. Why would fishermen be out in the monsoon? But she was tired. It had been a difficult night. She had popped in to see Inga in her chamber in the early hours. Jim, Gordo and the Bathroom Cockroach had come with her. Only Inga wasn't there. It was Diane and Alison locked into the decompression pod.

She had watched, helpless and horrified as they banged at the glass. 'Get us out of here! Get us out of here!' Diane had screamed soundlessly at them. Or 'Get it out of here!' Something was in there with her. Something small. Miranda had tried to get to the giant door to let them out, but it was like wading through treacle …

Miranda couldn't shake off the horror of the dream. And she knew she hadn't slept well. She and the cockroach had met in the bathroom at regular intervals during the night – still keeping to their no-contact pact. But she and Jim had visited Inga this morning. And found her well enough, if a bit fed up. Though she had some books. And her island lover was keeping a vigil outside her pod. Or was that a dream too? Jassie hadn't succeeded in rousing the doctor, but she had managed to leave a message for him at the Italian Island. They weren't getting any visitors from the mainland either. Their guests were stranded, unable to leave, and they were running out of beer.

Miranda had gashed her other foot on more thorns. The area around the clinic was not gardened very well. And of course, the gardeners, locals to a man, were still stuck off-island. Her leg looked like a shark had nibbled on it. Or lots of baby sharks.

Sponge Garden Reef was the dive destination of the day. It was pretty, but a tough and serious dive. Miranda still wished they wouldn't go out – especially not to a reef known for its swirling currents. After all, if nobody, not even the Islanders, understood what had pulled Inga down, how could they be sure it wouldn't happen again? But she had to acknowledge that there was really nothing to do on Small Island if you didn't dive.

It didn't have the distractions of the other islands. No gym, no squash court, no water-skiing, no parasailing. There were a few windsurfers, and an old abandoned pedalo tied up at high water mark, but that was about it. And that was wonderful in Miranda's eyes. The quiet beauty of the island was worth any amount of expensive and noisy toys as far as she was concerned. There wasn't even a disco. Unless the Al-Auddin party had disco facilities within their little palace. Hopefully not, though. Small Island was much too young for such things.

'Stay with the dive.' Jim always gave this little speech. 'Stick with your dive buddy, there's a whole ocean out there to get lost in.' This was big diving. It sorted out the adults from the fry, and Miranda wasn't the only one staying behind on the island.

Mal was on his own today. Todd wasn't listening. But there again, Todd knew everything already. There wasn't anything anyone could tell him. Miranda had to remind herself, yet again, that, without him, Inga wouldn't be as snug in her island pod as a hermit crab in a new shell. She would be gone. She would be out there – somewhere – in that blue and turquoise ocean. And the land here took enough bites out of you. Miranda didn't care to think what the sea might do if it chose.

Todd was watching Jassie, glorious in a scarlet and orange sarong, and the expression on his face made Miranda wonder, and not for the first time, how it was he never had any problem getting girlfriends. Surely it didn't take a lot of that vaunted feminine intuition to see how angry he was. How bitter.

He had a kind of impatient contempt towards Miranda, Alison, and, yes Diane. It was obvious he couldn't understand why Mal was wasting his time with her, and didn't like it that he was. But for girls like Inga and Jassie he ... Miranda found she couldn't define it.

So work on that, she told herself. What is writing but definition after all? It was anger, and longing too. But that didn't get it. It didn't begin to get it. Miranda was reminded of something else she had struggled and failed to define – the expressions on the face of the two young girls at Pattaya beach, as they looked at each other, across the elderly farangs they had in tow.

And why is it that men want to go with women who don't want to go with them, and who have to be paid to be charming? And why did Todd attract so many good looking single girls? And why was Inga suddenly pulled down into the depths? No. She was not going to think about that. Back to Todd. Her rescuer. No. No. No. She was not going to think about Inga. Not with Jim and his divers about to go back into the treacherous water. Inga was never attracted to Todd, anyway. Todd had no chance there. She liked the eager young Samir. He had nothing cynical about him.

Something had gone horribly wrong between the sexes. But what? Look as she might, she had never yet found a more convincing explanation than the one in Genesis. But who wanted to hear that these days?

Miranda sipped at her Coconut Cabana cocktail, and watched the boat disappear into the blue horizon. Now the whole day stretched before her. They wouldn't make it back till the evening. It had been interesting to meet Mrs Wolfie yesterday. She was a very brisk lady indeed. She had dealt with the Inga emergency with cool efficiency, but she obviously had no time to spend with non-diving wives. Miranda had gleaned – mainly from Trish – that her father was a business mogul from the mainland. He owned at least one island. Though not this one. Her mother was English. They had met on one of these white sand beaches. And they had divorced fairly quickly, so Jassie had apparently been brought up in the best of European boarding schools, dividing her holiday time between Switzerland, where her mother lived with her second husband, and these islands. It must have been an interesting upbringing and one that probably left her fairly self-reliant.

Her name was properly Jasodra – and she was tall and athletic, with exactly the colour of skin Inga was aspiring to tan to. She had almond-shaped brown eyes with dark brows and long lashes, masses of silky, curly dark hair, and a jolly hockey sticks personality to match. She had almost certainly been to the Swiss version of Roedean or some such place. The Shoal would be well cared for – bossed around, and given order marks if and when they swam out of line.

She had been brilliant in yesterday's emergency. As had everybody really. Miranda wondered why she still felt it was all somehow her fault? She walked back through the centre of the island, wondering if there was any chance of Gordo turning up. If he had been here, maybe it wouldn't have happened.

She was surprised by a faint sound of jingly music coming from behind the locked gates of Al-Auddin's walled compound. Or was it wind chimes jangling in the hot air? She had forgotten that the mysterious owner of Small Island had arrived. Surely that was a scent of musk or sandalwood wafting out – something stronger and spicier than the frangipani smells that bathed the little island. She longed to peer through the gates, but the thorns were clustering round it, and she wasn't going to get too close. Her leg was still stinging from last night.

She remembered that she and Jim were going to walk around and find the real entrance, the back door, or whatever. And if the Al-Auddin entourage had managed to get here then Gordo might be on his way at last. She would be so much happier once Gordo arrived.

Lying under an enormous sunshade, on hot white sand, with turquoise water swirling a few feet away, Miranda opened her book. Her holiday reading this year was proving almost too successful. She had brought the whole of Janet Frame's three part autobiography with her. It was unputdownable. It took her to another island, one much bigger and much colder, and to another country – the past. She lay under the shimmering Southland skies of New Zealand until shrieks and splashing pulled her slowly back to Small Island. So she wasn't alone. Of course. Diane and Alison! She hadn't seen them on the dive boat this morning. If Diane hadn't gone, then neither would Alison. They were dedicated beachies anyway, and probably preferred a sunbathing and snorkelling day, which would involve at least one swim around the house reef. On the deep ocean side.

They must have reached her little patch of beach. Well, she would go in too. She had her goggles and flippers. As she wasn't going to dive in them, she supposed she could call them that. She would swim across the lagoon, through the channel and surprise the girls. She didn't like to have the deep ocean under her, but as long as she could hug the reef and safety she would be OK. She might even swim round the island with them, if it seemed calm enough. And if there were no obvious sharks. Don't bother me, and I won't bother you.

The water was much clearer today, in spite of the continuing swell. She could see the sand and rocks and all their rainbow fish. It gave her confidence to know what was in the water with her. The sea in the channel was murky though, and swirly. It banged her against the reef side. Another festering scrape to add to the others. Think yourself lucky you didn't hit a stonefish, she told herself. She wouldn't live to regret that one. Stonefish disguise was near perfect. She had been snorkelling past bright corals one year, water as warm as a nice hot bath, and felt a chill of shock when one of the corals proved to be assessing her with a pair of sharp eyes.

Then suddenly she was through the channel. Alone with the deep ocean. And there was no sign of the giggling girls. Sounds must carry deceptively in the hot, wet air. There was no-one in the water. The ocean swelled in front of her, and Small Island stood softly behind her, little legs only just keeping its baby head above the waves. There was a blue nothingness beneath her, shading into blackness. And the large, soft sound of the water. Frightening to think of what lay beneath. But not to the divers presumably. Or the valiant snorkelers. Who were still nowhere in sight. Perhaps they had already surged past her, pulled by the current, which obligingly pulled you round and round the island till you chose your stopping off place.

Miranda looked down into the depths. She struggled to stay out of the current which flowed fast a few feet off the reef. She didn't want to risk going beyond it and becoming out of touch with the island itself. The ocean side of the house reef on Slightly Larger Island, the year before last, had been aglow with corals and sponges and their colourful inhabitants. But here was all blackness and blankness. And white too. The coral blanched in its death, became a skeleton of itself. A skeleton of a skeleton.

Jim had said something about the seas having got so hot during the summer that the corals near the surface had died. El Nino's fault apparently. Carmen's consort promptly snorkelled into her head, like a young Al Pacino, and he was blasting away at the corals with a machine gun.

All those coral gardens, just gone. How long had it taken them to form and grow? And what about the inhabitants? Had they died too? Or had they had to pack up and go? Had they moved downwards? Miranda looked into the immense ocean. What battles must have been fought down there as the top lot came down to find homes among the further-downers. It was dizzying. There was life down there though. After a certain point the reef got all knobbly and interesting once again. There were frondy things waving. It looked greeny blue, although if Jim photographed it, it would look quite different in the slides. She turned herself upside down and peered through the mask. Yes, there was colour down there and life. And fronds of green, wavering out into the water. Strangely.

A tiny golden fish, just the size of the occupant of the spare loo roll, dashed past her ears startling her, and Miranda decided she didn't want to be out there alone anymore. Already the effort of holding on against the current was telling, and she decided to snorkel back to the beach and resume her reading. The girls would find her after their swim. Probably. She would go back to New Zealand and the safety of the past.

The buffet that night was a bit of a disappointment. There was fish, plenty of it. And rice. And tropical fruits and creamy cake. But there was nothing much for the non-fish eaters, apart from pasta in an anonymous meaty sauce. There wasn't even the usual choice of fresh vegetables – just frozen carrots and tinned peas. But Mal's arrival to ask about the whereabouts of Diane halted the carping in its tracks.

If she wasn't back in their room, she usually met him in the sunset bar before dinner. But there was no sign of her in either place. Nor of Alison, as it turned out. Mal had gone straight off to the single-girl chalet when Miranda mentioned that she had seen them out snorkelling together off the house reef. 'Not like her to be late for her food,' he muttered as he left. And Miranda felt that, at some level, he feared losing her back into the world of single girls, and would rather she and Alison and Inga didn't socialize that much.

Not that Inga had been socializing with her friends. She had mainly been sitting at the staff table, whispering and giggling with her handsome young island man. And now they were alone together in the clinic, staring at each other through the glass of the decompression chamber.

Todd had just started to complain about the lack of steak and being reduced to fish-eating again, and Jim was mulling over the continuing absence of Gordo and any more divers, when Mal returned. There was no sign of either Alison or Diane. And it looked to him like they had never come back from their snorkel.

'It's OK, Mal,' Jim soothed, but he did look puzzled. 'They probably changed their minds and went island hopping instead. There are no shops off the reef you know.'

'Hey, there haven't been any boats in or out, apart from our dive boat. As far as I know.' Mal looked puzzled.

'Well, I saw them snorkelling earlier. I swam out to them. They were just off the channel.'

'When did you see them? Where?'

Miranda almost felt accused. Especially as she then had to change her statement, and admit that she hadn't in fact seen them at all. 'No. I heard them. This afternoon. Shouting and shrieking. They were just at the reef by our villa – you know where the sea channel is.'

'Shouting! What, calling for help?'

'No, of course not. They were just playing about. If it was them.' Why was everyone looking at her so accusingly?

'I did swim out, to join them. And say hello.' And I did, thought Miranda, straightaway.

'Because they sounded like they were in trouble?'

'Well, no, I mean I just heard them splashing round, and so I swam across the lagoon and out on to the other side to say hello. And have a look at the ocean.'

They were all watching her, expectantly. As if she was going to magic Diane and Alison out of her handbag just as she had earlier magicked marmalade and HP sauce.

'Well, I mean, I didn't see them … anyone … if it was them. I didn't see anyone. Or anything.'

Still they stared.

'There was nothing there. No-one.'

'This is a waste of time. We have to get Wolfie out with the boat. Now.' Mal strode off, Jim and Todd following.

'What's up, Miranda, you look like someone's died. Probably through lack of good red meat, may I say.' That was Patrick arriving with a plate of fish and coconuts.

Trish and Miranda sat in the sunset bar, each huddled over a large scotch. Coconut cocktails, stuffed with greenery and adorned with vulgar names didn't seem appropriate this evening. Jim, Wolfie and Jassie had organized search parties in all directions. Some on land, some on water. The land party, which included Trish and Miranda, had been all over the island, rushing in the heat, before full darkness came. The boat party was worryingly still out there. Somewhere.

'Wonderful English Samir speaks,' said Miranda vaguely into her cocktail. He had left his vigil beside the sleeping Inga and gone off with Wolfie on the big dive boat.

And then: 'They are looking for bodies, let's face it. And it'll be a miracle if they find those.'

'Oh, come on Miranda, the water's warm. You could survive a long time out there. They must have just got swept away somehow, but the boat will find them. Wolfie and the gang know all the currents there are.' Trish was a born comforter.

All sorts of things were running through Miranda's head. None of which seemed suitable to be let out of her mouth. Jim had never lost a diver. And she prayed he never would. The girls were snorkelling. They were not with the Shoal. And what happened to Inga was different. She was fine. She was still here, on Small Island.

And, after all, no-one could stop an ocean current grabbing someone. Whatever's happened, Diane and Alison were snorkelers, out on their own.

Miranda, don't say *were*, she whispered to herself. Say they *are* snorkelers. They are Diane and Alison. Nothing has happened to them. They were laughing and giggling. I know they were. She wished Jim were back. The last thought came out of her mouth. Rather woefully.

'Listen, Miranda, he's perfectly safe on the boat, with Wolfie. You know he is. And they'll be back soon. With the girls, I'm sure.'

'I wish Gordo had arrived though. He would be such a help now. I mean, will they have to dive, if they don't find ... you know ...?'

She would think about Gordo instead. He was younger than Jim, and happily married. It seemed that the current Mrs G would be the only Mrs G. Miranda thought back to hers and Jim's parents. Anything to keep her mind off what might have happened on Small Island. It was impossible to imagine them even contemplating a new wife or a new husband.

Especially so in the case of Jim's parents, who had called each other mum and dad. After all, whoever divorced their mother and father and got new ones. Although, come to think of it, hadn't there been a case, not so long ago, when a young child had gone to court to separate himself from his parents and had succeeded in effectively divorcing them? No, nothing was certain anymore. Except the fact that Alison and Diane were missing. All trains of thought seemed to end up there.

'Look! The search party.' Inga sat up briskly. Miranda brightened for a moment, thinking the boat that held Jim was back, but it was the party that Mal had organized. The girls and the staff were going to search the island from top to toe again. Even though it was now dark. Mal had gone to rout out such members of staff as he could find, and had arrived back with the omelette chef, who looked very sleepy, poor guy. Mo the waiter was with him. And Mo the Boathook, the youngest of the Mo's. He looked tense and jumpy. Almost furtive. He didn't know something he wasn't telling, did he?

They had searched the whole island. More than half the villas were empty and shuttered. And they had already been inside every Shoal occupied villa. Jassie had been round the kitchens, before Wolfie, Jim and Elder Mo left in the dive boat. The shops were still closed, as most of the islanders were stranded out there somewhere. And there was no-one but themselves and the staff in the bar and dining room. This was just displacement activity. Anything to stop them facing up to what must have happened.

'What exactly did you hear?' Mal asked for the millionth time.

Miranda thought back to the day, which now seemed more remote and strange than her tropical dreams. 'Nothing. I didn't hear anything.'

'But you did, Miranda, you said so.' That was Jassie, at her most Head Prefect-ish.

'I know. I mean splashing, shrieking, nothing useful.'

'Yes, but think, Miranda. Think. Shrieking. Did it sound like they were in trouble?'

'No', Miranda replied, for the millionth time. 'It was just shouting, you know, playing around. Giggling. Yes, I think they were laughing.'

'But why did you go straight in the water and out there? You must have thought something.'

I did, thought Miranda. But she didn't know how to say it. Her only thought when she had heard them was that she ought to go and be sociable and do the requisite amount of splashing and shrieking herself. And now she couldn't be sure what she had heard. And what she had seen. Well, she hadn't seen them. That was clear. She hadn't seen anything. And she could remember … no, she couldn't remember exactly what she heard, but she couldn't remember any sense of urgency or panic in her swimming out to join them.

But why did she think it was them? What made her assume it?

Because, Miranda told herself, apart from the skeleton staff, who would not have had time to shriek and play round the reef, and Inga who was locked in her pod, there was only her and the girls on the island.

Miranda wished the word 'skeleton' hadn't entered her consciousness at all.

She put her drink down rather forcefully, for quiet Miranda. 'I assumed it was them. Playing around on the reef. But it can't have been. Because when I swam over they weren't there.'

'Yes, but Miranda …' This was Trish, trying to soothe. 'I think what Mal means is can you think of anything else? I mean did you have a good look round when you got there? Not that any of us can blame you if you didn't. After all, there wasn't any reason for you to think you should do.'

Kind Trish was ready to excuse Miranda for whatever negligence on her part might have led to the disappearance of two Shoalies.

'Trish. I didn't have to *really look*. It's Small Island, remember? I swam just beyond the reef, and there was no-one there. It obviously wasn't them I heard. I expect it was just birds or something.'

But even as she said it, it felt wrong. Not like birds at all. But not like someone in trouble either. And in any case, it didn't help, as Mal pounced on the idea of birds and began to worry it to death. Just as if he thought they might have been carried off by a giant albatross.

How beautiful Small Island was after dark. The moon was beginning to glint on the frill of a wave – helped out by the leaping gleam of fish. There were little Dalek lights at odd intervals, with pools of soft darkness in between, and moon glinting on fallen frangipani blossom. Their fragrance filled the hot night. But so did the thought that something had happened to Diane and Alison, some small disaster, while out snorkelling, within only metres of safety, which meant that they would never see this again. And that couldn't be. It simply couldn't. Their story was so unfinished, so undecided. How could they have disappeared, completely without drama? Right in the middle of everything. Almost before they had got started.

Death couldn't have come just like that, could it? And surely no-one could have ended their lives in such an un-dramatic way in the vicinity of Carmen? Which was the only useful thought the woman had so far supplied.

Miranda wondered if this was another of her tropical nightmares and if she would wake up in a moment in their villa with Jim beside her, and all the Shoal safe in their beds. The Bathroom Cockroach would be tucked away in his loo roll home, and the topsy-turvy world put to rights again.

Mal had got them all organized. He had insisted on another search, even though it was now dark. Still dark and Wolfie and Jim weren't back yet. So what, Miranda told herself sharply, they have a lot of looking to do. And anyway Jassie was back at the dive centre, talking to them even now. She was trying to make contact with the nearest resort and shopping island, just in case the girls had caught a passing boat, in spite of the weather. She ought to worry about Mal, who had bravely insisted on walking round the beach. Looking for anything – and don't even think *anyone* – anything that might have washed up. Because that small fierce tide was coming in.

Patrick, Trish and Mo the waiter would check all the chalets again. Even the empty ones this time. They would try the doors, look inside, bang about a bit. Young Mo was taking the small boat out to go round the lagoon. He took his boathook. Samir and Jassie were going to go through the emptied staff quarters with a fine toothed comb just as soon as Jassie had raised the other island. Or given up trying to. And Miranda and Todd found they had been delegated to walk through the centre of the island. Alone together.

Todd was obviously as thrilled to be with Miranda as she was with him. They didn't speak. He intimidated by his silences, and Miranda was determined to beat him at his own game there. If it was up to her to speak first, she resolved, they would go through the centre of the island in total silence. At least it would mean they could really concentrate on looking. Although how could anyone hide on Small Island even if they wanted to?

Todd wasn't even pretending to look, as if he knew for sure it would be no use. He was walking briskly and impatiently, obviously longing to be in more congenial company. Whatever had been on his mind seemed to have been sorted.

Did he know something about the girls? Had he seen them go off somewhere?

Unfortunately for her resolve, Miranda's thought came straight out of her mouth. 'I wonder if they just got on to a boat and went island hopping, like Jim said. They would have got stranded there with this storm carrying on. And you know so many lines of communication are down. They couldn't contact us. That must be it.' She turned to Todd with real hope in her eyes. 'You see, at least one boat must have got in because the Al-Auddin's have arrived. The guy who owns the island. You know? There were people in the compound yesterday. Well … not people, but music and lights and things. Look!'

They had arrived at the walled villa, but Miranda's triumphant pointing was premature. It was as quiet and shuttered as when she and Jim had first seen it. And the gate was so thick with thorns that Miranda wondered how they had ever got their glimpse into the flagged courtyard beyond without being skewered. She rubbed thoughtfully at her injured legs. Todd raised his eyebrows. 'That's for the stewardesses.' Stewardesses were one of the few subjects on which he could get quite animated.

'No, Todd, it isn't. Jim and I thought so. Although I did wonder about its being so far from the airport, but Jim asked one of the Mo's and he said that it belonged to Mr Al–'

Todd interrupted her, in a manner both brisk and weary that intimated she wasn't worth Todd wasting his words on, but some things just had to be put right.

'This Aladdin guy owns it. And he brings his family here sometimes.

But he also has some favourite stewardesses. Kapish? And has he brought a couple of blonde babes out this time! Not at the same time as the wives. Obviously.'

'Has he?' asked Miranda wonderingly, not realizing that Todd wasn't asking a question.

He raised his eyebrows scathingly, but left it at that. She realized that he would admire such conduct, and wish to think that was how the elusive Mr Al-Auddin conducted his business, even if it wasn't. Miranda wished that she had stuck to her resolve not to speak unless he spoke to her.

If this was truly Aladdin's island, oughtn't she be allowed three wishes? If he would grant her a wish, she would wish for the girls to turn up. Right now. Or that they would send us a message from the Club Thirties Island or something. She wouldn't care how mad that made Mal, if only they were alright – that she, Miranda, hadn't failed them in some way. But they had sounded fine. They weren't calling for help or anything. If it was them she had heard.

The emptiness of the Al-Auddin palace had worried her. She knew she always got a bit confused in the tropics, had strange dreams, slept in the day, awoke at night, but they had both seen people there, her and Jim. No. Get it right Miranda! They had heard music and seen lights. They had seen signs of people last night. The palace had looked like it was inhabited. And she knew what she hadn't seen. She hadn't seen Diane and Alison.

'You mean you saw some girls arrive?' The implications of what Todd had just said suddenly hit her.

But Todd was lighting up yet another cigarette and declined to answer. If there was something on his mind, he wasn't telling Miranda. All too soon the central path ran out and they were walking between the villas back to the sea. Soon they would meet up with Mal, and the others. Thankfully. But there was only the moonlight, glinting on the waves. The swell had got bigger, rushing up the beach to the very edge of the mangroves. Miranda watched Todd, who was savagely stamping at an advance party of thorns that had erupted on to the path. 'I think the cleaners and gardeners are still stranded by the storm. They usually keep up the islands so well.'

Why did she have to say that? Why did she have to feel guilty and apologetic because there were some thorns growing on a small tropical island that Todd happened to be on? It was no use though, and Miranda found herself wittering on about how tidy these islands were kept, about how the leaves were usually swept up, the sand combed, the insects tidied away. She was being intimidated by his silence after all. She was apologizing for the weather now! And what was the point of that. Better to say nothing more till the others came. Let them deal with him.

What strange contrasts America produced. People as open and friendly as Mal. Or as closed-off as Todd. And it wasn't shyness, or insecurity, or ... well, anything Miranda could understand. Beyond a kind of rage. But it was a cold anger. Cold as ... She couldn't come up with anything better than the Blackadderish 'an extremely cold thing'. A novelist would have to do better than that, said work-Miranda, stern in her head. And where was Carmen, now that she actually had some use for her? Because don't tell me she couldn't deal with Todd. In fact, wouldn't she be just Todd's sort of woman?

She watched his profile. Yes. He really was very good-looking. And he'd certainly be photogenic, so he'd do for Carmen. But Miranda wouldn't want to be alone with him anywhere else in the world but Small Island. Because the islands were as safe as houses. Except that two of them weren't here now. And don't most accidents take place in the home?

Her mind went back to the lagoon, the voices, her swim across it. There was no-one there. Definitely. No big fish. No threshing in the water. No screaming. Not that sort of scream anyway. Poor Mal. He had the worst search. Because, if something had happened to Alison and

Diane while they were snorkelling, then surely there would be something, some clue on the beach. Maybe even …

As if on cue, Mal appeared from the mangroves, looking a bit battered and damp. But relieved. 'Nothing,' he said. 'Nothing. And I've been right round. How about you?'

'Nothing, Bud,' said Todd, almost effusively. 'No sign of them.'

Miranda felt that the message was clear. There was nothing wrong with Todd. He could and would chat away when there was someone around worth talking to. She almost felt like saying she felt the same. Start a big row. Anything to keep her mind off Alison and Diane, who, anyway, were stranded out there on some island. They would be at the bar even now, surrounded by gorgeous young men. That was the only possibility. And, as for the voices she had heard, they were beginning to sound in her memory more and more like the harsh cries of the black crows that would sometimes knock the glasses off the veranda tables.

Thank You God, Thank You God. It was Wolfie, Samir and Jim back with the dive boat. For a moment it almost seemed to Miranda that everything was fine again. But they had no Diane and Alison with them, and no news of them. They hadn't been able to make it to the nearest Resort Island. The waves had warned them that the storm was returning so they had cut back to Small Island.

THE FOURTH DAY

Gordo! She was not all alone at Shark Point, suddenly so dark and cold. Gordo had come to get her. His teeth gleaming as white as Carmen's in the black water, welcoming little fishes in with gently smiling jaws. And now he was reaching out to welcome her. Reaching out and out and out. Why was he trying to pull her down? Into those black depths? All his long, wavering green arms ...

Miranda sat up. Jim slept, exhausted beside her. What time is it, she thought, dazedly. 2.30. She could see Jim's travel alarm gleaming faintly in the dark. Green, like the wavering arms on the reef.

'JIM!'

'What the ...?' Startled Jim sat up.

'Jim. I did see something on the reef. I did.'

'What ...?' He was still asleep, although his eyes were open, and he stared at her in confusion, before falling back into sleep instantly. She didn't have the heart to wake him again. Not after the hours of worry on the boat. There was no point anyway. She could tell him in the morning. About the wavering green she had seen coming from the depths of the reef, where a few moments before she had heard Diane and Alison shrieking and shouting.

'Miranda, you were dreaming. And I'm not blaming you, after yesterday. This trip is turning into a nightmare in itself.' Jim towelled himself vigorously.

'No, Jim, truly, I did see it. It was green and wavering and it wasn't till I saw it in this dream ... And you said, you told me. Blood underwater looks green. Green.'

'Miranda. It's been a terrible strain on all of us. I just can't believe we've lost them. And in fact, I don't think we have. I'm sure they have gone off to another island, where they thought there would be a singles bar and all the rest of it. And they are stuck there. You know most communication is still down.'

'No, Jim, Diane wouldn't go without Mal. She wouldn't just go off. If she did – and she wouldn't – she'd at least leave a note or something.'

'Oh no?' Jim was looking a bit smug and mysterious. 'Well, it might interest you to know that Mal admitted he and Diane had had one hell of a row the night before.'

'Mal and Diane rowing? Not them as well. Were they all at it that night?'

'Oh yes, they were rowing alright. Mal might be with Diane, but she is not at all sure that she is with him to the same extent. He wants commitment. She doesn't. Their usual row. But there's something about being together on a small island ...'

'Yes, but ...' Miranda realized that she had simply taken it for granted that Diane would be receptive to Mal's charms in the end. He was sought after among the single girls after all. She had failed to take Gil into account. Failed to take Diane herself into account. She had been assuming that because she was single girl, she wanted to get married asap.

'So, she might well have gone off just to teach him a lesson. Or perhaps she got bored, and wanted to meet someone else to add a bit more complication her life. And whatever other island they are on, they will be stranded there till this thing blows itself out.'

'But, Jim ...' Miranda's voice trailed off. She wanted to say that she had heard them, shrieking and giggling. At least, she had thought it was giggling. And she had seen those fronds of green wavering up from the black ocean depths. But suddenly she wasn't sure anymore.

It was all taking on the aspect of a dream. She had had night after night of vivid and rather horrible dreams since she arrived on Small Island and it was getting a bit hard to tell the fact from the fiction now. Perhaps it was all her fault, for bringing that Carmen here with her. She was enough to give anyone nightmares.

Still, morning had come, as it always does. Bringing the usual breakfast buffet. Well, not the usual breakfast buffet in fact, as most of the staff were still stranded off-island and the supply boats hadn't got in. Miranda was OK. There were chapattis. Towers of them, hot and warm and soft. And yogurt in its silver bowl. And a fish curry, left over from last night. And a green curry, made of some rather stringy ladies' fingers. Okra, thought Miranda. Somehow, this morning, I prefer the American word. But there was toast too. And the omelette chef still manned his giant pan. And there were even the usual boiled eggs for feeding the fish.

The Shoal ate together. Smaller now, perhaps they would cling a bit closer for comfort. But Patrick and Trish didn't seem to be speaking to each other, or anyone. Mal was restless, unable to eat, jumping up and down, and constantly asking if there had been any sightings, any messages. Wolfie and Jassie didn't join them. And Miranda missed their common sense reassurances.

'But what about their mobile phones?' She suddenly remembered that Alison was never seen without hers back home, and there had been speculation that Diane kept hers glued to her ear even while she was asleep.

'What about service providers?' said Todd caustically and Miranda wished she had kept her thoughts to herself. She usually ended up wishing that when Todd was around. Whatever did Jim see in the guy?

Her conscience pricked her as she remembered Inga and the heroic rescue. Could I, Miranda, have done that? Could I really have plunged down after her? But even if I had, I would not have known what to do. And Inga would have been in those wavering green arms. Perhaps Todd's scorn was fair enough really. Should she tell Mal about the green in the water? No. It would be cruel. And after all, what had she seen down there. It was only in the dream, or she would have told him yesterday.

'We've never had communication problems on the islands before. This must be the mother of all storms.' That was Todd, picking irritably at his cheeseless omelette.

'The weather's strange all over the world now,' Miranda remarked, instantly forgetting her resolve never to talk to him unless she absolutely had to.

The look he gave her – or rather the look he didn't give her – was masterful in its eloquence. She was obviously the sort of person who went on about global warming, the look said. And it was witheringly clear what he thought of that sort of person.

Actually, I'm not, Miranda wanted to say. But it was hard to reply to an accusation that hadn't, strictly speaking, been made. And indeed she wasn't. She wasn't at all sure she believed in it. In spite of the shrinking sand spit their helicopter had landed on, in spite of the waves that beat against the tiny beaches of Small Island. For sure, the weather seemed to be changing, but surely the forces behind the weather were infinitely more old and powerful and mysterious than science had yet to acknowledge. However, it had to be a good idea for them to try to stop polluting the earth. And ruining it. Yes. She would support that with all her heart. In theory.

But in practice? How? Because here we are, thought Miranda, watching the Shoal at their omelettes, watching the left-overs pile up on their plates. She thought guiltily of the Niagara-like shower she had taken this morning, and would be taking again tonight. Would she be prepared to come here if there was only fish, rice and coconuts to eat; the sea to bathe in and a hole in the ground for a loo? Jim would be. Wolfie probably was. And, to be fair, Todd would. And the island men would cope. But most of the tourists would not.

'If the weather is still so bad, then how come boats got in yesterday?' That was Mal worrying away, and longing for someone to tell him that boats had come and gone all day and that Diane had been seen waving goodbye from one of them.

'Boats got in.' That was Todd very definite. 'And I know, because I saw the old guy who owns this place, well, his boat anyway. And it was unloading some gorgeous blonde stewardesses for that palace of his.'

That can't be right, thought Miranda, thinking of the thorny and shuttered gates that she and Todd had walked past on that dreadful search last night. Nobody had been through those gates for a hundred years. But then she remembered that she and Jim had decided there must be another way in. A back door. They had meant to go and have a look for it. She wasn't going to ask Todd though. She would have to explore herself later. As for boatloads of blonde stewardesses, that was surely a Todd fantasy. She wasn't the only one having strange tropical dreams.

'Look, Mal,' Jim was trying to stop Mal from paying his tenth visit to the office. 'As soon as anyone hears from them we'll know. And it will be OK. You don't just disappear off an island like this. Leaving no trace. Out in the deep ocean, off the dive boat, yes, it could happen ... but not off this island. You heard what Todd said. A boat did get in yesterday. Anybody could have called by here during the day. In fact, has anyone seen the Al-Auddin yacht anywhere?' Jim sounded both relieved and triumphant.

Of course we haven't thought Miranda. Hurray.

'What do you mean? There's no boat here, apart from the dive boats.'

'Exactly. He must have landed his catch – sorry to be so sexist, ladies – had a look round and sailed off again. And guess who hitched a lift with him. In fact it was probably the stewardesses that Miranda heard yesterday snorkelling.'

Miranda began to wish she had kept her tales of snorkelers to herself. Because the point still remained she had heard voices, but no-one had been where the voices came from by the time she swam there. She could no longer even hear what the voices had sounded like in her head. But the wavering ribbons of green seemed to loom larger and larger, with an unwelcome persistence.

It wasn't till later in the morning that it was realized that the small boat was missing. And Young Mo with it. This day was turning into a nightmare re-run of the day before.

Once more the search parties went out. On land and on sea. Wolfie and the dive boat crew went in search of their missing comrade, while Jassy manned the communications and tried to raise any and all islands she could. The mainland was still cut off, as were most of the local islands. And nobody reported any sightings of Mo, Alison or Diane. The Al-Auddin yacht had not been seen anywhere but, briefly, at Small Island – if the Todd version could be trusted. Nor could they offer any help. They had their own problem. They too had holidaymakers marooned, way past their sell-by date. And they too were running out of food.

This time Miranda and Jim walked round the beach while others searched inland. Ali the Omelette and Mo the Chef reported that Mo the Younger's bed had not been slept in. They didn't seem worried though. Relieved if anything. And she also remembered how edgy Young Mo had been yesterday. Something was up. But what?

Lunchtime came and went, but no-one noticed.

When they gathered in the small restaurant that evening, the gorgeous buffets of earlier in the week had shrunk to fish, rice, coconuts, a few frozen veggies, and some powdery instant pudding. Everybody pushed the food listlessly around the plates, said little and went off to bed early. Looking back at the table, Miranda saw that they seemed to have wasted as much food as usual. If not more.

Jim and Miranda held hands under the glorious night sky of Small Island. The air was heady with perfume. Crickets sang louder than the birds of the day. The sun may have put its night cap on, but it was still deliriously hot and steamy. The island was full of joy, seeming to contradict the bleakness of the empty spaces at the Shoal's table. Was it really going to be alright after all?

As they passed the palace of Al-Auddin, Miranda remembered Inga.

'Jim. Let's go and see how Inga is. I don't even know if anyone took her any dinner!'

'Oh, that's OK. She's un-podded now. Jassie has been letting her out at regular intervals. Even though we haven't got a doctor out here yet. She'll be with Samir. She'll have to go back in the chamber tonight though. And for at least some of tomorrow.'

'Oh. Good.' Miranda was relieved. 'I should think she and Samir ate with the staff. It was probably a lot more exciting than what we had tonight.'

'Ah.'

They walked on through the soft night, quiet, thinking. Wondering and worrying.

THE FIFTH DAY

Miranda slept on, while Jim and Mal snorkelled in the early morning lagoon, as the night creatures went to their beds in the coral, and the morning fish began to wake up and patrol. If anything momentous had recently happened, just off the reef, they found no trace of it. Meanwhile Miranda struggled on through thorns, following the cockroach round and round. They had to find something. A palace. They had to find it. But it was too small for them. They should have looked before. They could hear them calling but they couldn't get through. 'Stop, stop ...' It was trying to push her through. She didn't want to. She couldn't fit. She would wait for Gordo – he'd be out here somewhere with Jim.

'Stop, Jim, don't push ...'

'It's nearly lunchtime, Miranda, come on. You've been asleep for hours.' He shook her back to the fifth day. Sunlight was streaming into the room.

'What ...?' She couldn't even remember getting up in the night. 'I must have slept well. What time is it?'

'I told you. Lunchtime, nearly. We've been for a swim in the lagoon. Come on.'

'Inga? Diane and Alison?' It came back to her in its vivid horror. 'I nearly got to them ...' Her voice tailed away with the fragments of her dream.

'Inga is fine, remember? And Diane and Alison will be fine too. We should hear something today.'

'But Mo. Where's Mo?' A feeling of guilt, something left over from the dream ... had they remembered to look for him? Her and the cockroach? No. But they hadn't been looking for anyone, they had been looking for a gate, a door, something … Miranda shook her head to clear it and set off for the bathroom. Her dream buddy was absent she was happy to note. She felt as if they were spending altogether too much time together.

The Shoal had somehow, wordlessly, agreed to meet up in the sunset bar before lunch. They clutched their bottles of water, bought at breakfast, and stared out to sea. Miranda did the same, once she had assured herself that no-one had spotted anything terrible floating in the lagoon. The bar opened up mid-morning, with Ali the Omelette officiating, and served coffee and Banana Mananas. Had it been an ordinary day, Miranda would have sat at the corner table, which was shaded and which caught a breeze off the sea, and corrected a few proofs, and daydreamed, and enjoyed the beauty of the little island and the glory of its turquoise lagoon. Perhaps Carmen would have turned up.

A fat lot of use the woman had been last night when they were all searching. Although the word 'fat' should never be used in the same sentence as her heroine. Not if Miranda wanted to sell her to Hollywood.

Mal paced up and down. He wanted to be out there. Searching. He now seemed more angry than worried. Miranda could only hope that he was right. Jim had reported that there was no sign of life at the Al-Auddin villa, and no sign of the Al-Auddin yacht. It therefore seemed clear that there had been enough of a lull for him to come and go, and that Diane and Alison had gone with him. Todd sat clutching a cigarette and a beer from the fridge in his villa. He looked cynical, and his body language said, *I told you so.*

As for Mo, Samir was inclined to think he might have just quietly taken the boat and driven it home. He had never been happy about spending the nights on the island anyway. And there was no sign of wreckage, or anything. Patrick and Trish had just come back from visiting Inga. She was fine, Trish assured them, as she rubbed distractedly at a slash on her leg. She was a bit fed up, still having to return to her pod at regular intervals, but relieved to hear about the Al-Auddin boat.

Samir hadn't been there, he was on kitchen duty due to the shortage of staff, but he would soon return. And Jassie was there when he wasn't. She was a qualified hyperbaric nurse, along with all her other accomplishments. This marriage was certainly turning out to be a suitable one.

Unfortunately the news seemed to irritate Todd. And Miranda quickly pressed the delete button in her head as he wondered where the doctor had got to.

'He's still stuck with Gordo and the German divers on the mainland. He was on his way back from a Dive Medic Conference in Basle.' Jim had got all this from Wolfie and Jassie.

'Well, stay healthy, folks,' said Patrick downing a large whisky.

Trish looked disgusted. But not about the doctor situation. Miranda didn't think she had even taken it in. Miranda felt sure he was doing it to upset Trish. It might be better if she just ignored it. Or even poured one for herself, if she could face it. So sad they were still fighting. On Paradise Island too. But, if the problem was children as Jim thought, there was no resolution. Yet it seemed they did love each other. They should have met when they were both much younger and had their children together. An impossible situation. Miranda suddenly remembered that it was the dream Trish and Patrick who loved each other. What they really felt she had no idea.

The day drifted along. Every so often someone would make to go snorkelling, and awkwardly decide not to. Jassie had returned to ask if they would mind lunching at the bar today as they were so short of staff that they didn't want to open the dining hall. She, Wolfie and Samir joined them over their plates of fish, rice and coconuts. There would be no dive this afternoon as they had to do some technical work on the boat.

'What are our chances of getting off the island?'

It was Jim who asked what had been on all their minds.

97

Wolfie assured them that the storm would almost certainly be over by tomorrow. The island boat could take them to the little sand spit out there in the ocean and the helicopter would be able to come for them as planned. 'No problem.'

'But what about Diane? And Alison …? How can we leave without them, without knowing where they are?' worried Miranda.

'Jassie's got through to the Italian island. They are putting the word out to watch for the Al-Auddin yacht.'

'I can't believe Diane would just go off like that.' Mal shook his head, and looked grimly into his beer. Miranda agreed with Mal. But, she asked herself, if they haven't vanished with Aladdin, then where are they?

Jim jumped up. 'Surely we aren't going to let an island day go by without a proper dive.' He chivvied Todd and Mal.

'Hey, hold it Jimbo. We're flying tomorrow remember. At least I hope we are.'

'No we aren't. We've got another full day. And then it's not till the evening. We can do a dive now. Just off the house reef. We won't go deep or anything anyway.'

Funny. It wasn't like Todd to get his days mixed up. That's more my style, thought Miranda. Perhaps the tropics were beginning to get to him too. It showed she wasn't the only one who didn't want to linger here, in spite of stewardesses being on the island! She could see that the idea of a dive appealed to Mal though. And she knew why. Out there, off the house reef, was where Diane was last seen. If Miranda was a reliable witness. Last heard, she meant. Last heard. Whatever else, she was completely sure she didn't see them. Might they find something at this late stage? Shuddering, Miranda hoped not. Let us go on hoping, she begged the small island. Please.

Miranda swam beyond the current. She had been deeply unhappy at the thought of them diving beyond the reef. And just as unhappy at the thought of waiting back on the beach. Wondering. And not knowing. If you can't beat them join them. She had decided to snorkel just above the divers. She could see what was happening then. For all this talk of boats, and other islands, the uncomfortable fact was that the last sightings of Mo, Louise and Diane were by the house reef. Almost exactly where Jim had picked to do their dive.

The current was the problem. To keep right out of it, she had to move a bit further out into the ocean than she liked. It wasn't so easy to get back to the island from here. And this was just the spot where she had heard Diane and Alison. Thought I heard them, she corrected herself, as she watched Jim and Mal, Patrick and Todd buddy up and check each other's air and regulators. The sea was calm though. As calm as it had been the day they arrived. And was that really only five days ago! Soon the divers would disappear under this calm water, but Miranda should be able to see them. Trish wasn't going to join them. She had a headache and had decided to have a restful afternoon on the beach. She had been lying out in the sun, toasting herself to an even deeper shade of brown as they waded out into the lagoon.

'I hope you're wearing a good sunscreen, Trish,' Miranda had called back as they set off.

'Stop clucking, Miranda.' Jim thought his Shoal were old enough to decide for themselves in these matters.

Wolfie and Samir were doing things to the dive boat this afternoon, and Jasodra was still trying to raise any and all other islands to try to find the missing snorkelers. She and Wolfie had been very dismissive of the idea that Mr Al-Auddin had been and gone. 'He may own that villa,' Jassie had said, 'but he never comes out here. He's got homes all over the place. And they're all much grander than this one.' But Wolfie did admit that he could have offered it to a friend, they could have called by on an island cruise. Apparently no special arrangements were needed should he come. He brought his own staff and his own supplies – even his own water.

She pulled herself back to the moment. Because she was beginning to drift alarmingly. Literally. She needed to watch where she was in relation to the house reef. Could that be what happened to Diane and Alison, she wanted to ask the divers in their underwater world. Could they simply have got a little bit too far off and drifted away?

Suddenly it seemed so likely. And dreadful in that case that they were wasting time up here when they should be out with boats and helicopters. But the weather was still such that the helicopters and seaplanes would be grounded. Small Island was bathed in sunlight, but it was ringed by dark clouds standing off at the horizon; and were the waves getting bigger? No, she told herself, it's almost miraculously calm round Small Island. Almost as if it wants us to have our last dives.

She smiled, imaging the tiny island holding up its baby hand and telling the waves to Stop! Or perhaps the storm itself would pass gently over the little toddler island. She floated, staring up at the sky. There was a golden edge to the land, some of the palms were glowing, turned to new copper by the sun. It was almost too bright. Something about the saturated colours worried Miranda. The clouds were like curtains drawn back, all the light was concentrated on the stage of Small Island – waiting for the next act of the drama?

She began to watch the weather anxiously, wondering how she could best warn the divers if the storm suddenly struck.

'SHARK!'

Miranda jerked upright in panic and almost sank. Jim had suddenly appeared on the surface, a few yards off, splashing and spluttering. He was being attacked! Oh God, please help us. He is being pulled down by a shark, right in front of me. Miranda swam. She must get to Jim. She must get to Jim. But it was like swimming through treacle. She could not go fast enough. And time seemed to have slowed itself down, gloatingly. She would go for its eyes – its sharky eyes. It would have to let go.

She found herself looking to see if Gordo and the Bathroom Cockroach were swimming alongside her. But it was no dream. There was only a fat little golden fish whirring through the water ahead of her face – the gentle waves, the island, and Jim splashing frantically at the surface. He was trying desperately to get to her. And, horror upon horror, this must be what happened to Diane and Alison. They must have been screaming to me for help. As Jim is now.

But.. Thank God. Thank God. Jim was still up and swimming and coming towards her. After long, long moments, they met in the water. And grabbed each other.

'Shark, Miranda.' Jim spluttered, his mouth full of water. 'Beautiful! Did you see it? I didn't want you to miss it. Look! Down there.'

Dazed, Miranda stared into the waters and saw the bottom of a large shark disappearing into the depth. It was retreating as fast as if it had been propelled by one of Carmen's size 9 feet.

'He says I shouldn't be scared of the water, and then he does that to me!' Miranda accepted a large gin and tonic gratefully. They had made it back safely from the dive, after all, and it seemed that everyone on the island had met up at the sunset bar. Jassie, Wolfie, and Elder Mo were at the next table. Ali the Omelette was manning the bar. What a long day the omelette cook put in! Patrick and Trish were on their way, and Todd and Mal had drawn a bit apart talking intensely about something.

They were discussing the Aladdin boat, Miranda thought, from the odd word she was able to detect over the roar of the fans. Mal would want every single detail, every possible reassurance.

Miranda couldn't make any sense of it though. Try as she might. Those stewardesses. Where were they? Had they come and gone within the space of an hour or so? And what about Inga and Samir? The last thought came out of her mouth.

'Jassie and Wolfie had a bit of a disagreement about that. He thinks she should say there till the doctor comes. I think Jassie has sneaked her out this evening, but she won't come to the bar and upset Wolfie.'

Miranda gulped at her gin and tonic. She would get it down quickly and return to the boring old Banana Manana. She was not a great drinker. The visionary nice cups of tea of middle-age floated through her head. But you weren't allowed to be middle-aged now. You had to be 'hot' and glamorous whatever your age. Carmen and Al Nino stayed away. There was nothing here to interest them. And middle-age and Carmen could never meet up. Al could probably get as old as he liked and still creak off into the sunset with the girl. But Carmen couldn't. What a strain it all was.

'Anyway,' Jim put down his beer decisively, 'I don't know how many times I've told you to ignore all this hysteria about sharks. Just don't bother them. Keep an eye on them, make sure you're not worrying them. Don't act like a dying fish, and you'll have no aggro from them.'

'Miranda, You are like a dying duck in a thunderstorm. Always daydreaming. Wake up girl!' Those strictures, surfacing from her distant childhood, weren't reassuring. Could a shark fairly be expected to tell the difference between a dying fish and a dying duck? The tropical night moved on. The moon lit up the water, and the stars wheeled glowingly round. After a while the Shoal began to drift away from the bar. They had eaten. Someone – Jassie probably? – had made popcorn. And there were some crisps. There was little talk. People seemed eager to leave. To go to bed and sleep.

But they were almost furtive about it. As if they felt guilty about sleeping comfortably while two of their number might be out there, somewhere, maybe in desperate need of help. Even Jim looked tired, and, after downing a last double, he agreed that they might as well go to bed.

Miranda was glad. She wanted nothing more than to sleep and forget for a few hours. They could do nothing till the morning anyway, and who knew if Diane and Alison might not be back by then. The whole thing was probably a misunderstanding. They had left a message with one of the staff, he had forgotten to give it, something like that. They had simply succumbed to the temptation to island-hop with Al-Auddin.

Perhaps he really was Aladdin, with a magic carpet. Tropical storms, no matter how fierce, wouldn't upset the carpet flying schedules.

Miranda braced herself for her dreams, which seemed to be getting more and more feverish. And she prepared herself to wake up for innumerable bathroom trips during the night. But tonight she couldn't even get to sleep. The wind had fallen, as Wolfie had promised it would, and she could hear voices, low, angry and bitter in the chalet next door. There was no relief till midnight, when the wind got up again and the wild sea restored a kind of calm to the island.

THE SIXTH DAY

'Miranda! Wake up!' Jim was shaking her, and there was a clattering and screaming at the door.

I knew it was all a dream, she thought vaguely. 'It isn't Gordo Jim, it's just the rain.' Gordo would hardly turn up at this late stage. Even if he could. What would be the point? There were no diving days left. Miranda sat up. What was Jim doing in her Gordo dream? Didn't she and Gordo have to go and find him first? And they never did. And there really was a clattering and shouting at the door.

This is getting ridiculous. She felt around for the bedside light switch, and clicked it on to find Jim, wrapped in a hasty towel, opening the door to a hysterical Trish. What had been happening in the villa next door? She and Pat must have had their most dreadful, perhaps final row. And she'd stormed out. Or maybe even he, sunny Patrick, had thrown her out!

'Miranda! '

Trish's words began to penetrate through her sleep haze. 'He's dead. I think he's dead. Come quickly. He's not breathing. Hurry up.'

Jim was dashing into his shorts, heedless of Trish being there. She was white and shaking. Wearing nothing but a slender strapped red silk nightdress, with dark wet patches on the front. Some of the wet pattern on Trish's nightdress transferred itself on to Jim's shorts and bare chest.

'Where is he Trish?' that was Jim.

'The bathroom. Hurry. He isn't breathing.' Trish suddenly swayed and Jim caught her.

Trish was icy cold. Of course! The air conditioning. 'I'll turn the air con off, Trish. And the fan. That'll warm you. And the kettle. Just let me get the kettle on.'

She looked at her hands to make sure the nightdress hadn't spread there too. Perhaps she should wash them anyway. What a good thing all those stains weren't green, or she might have thought it was blood. The world 'blood' and the cold water running over Miranda's hands woke her up fully. Trish was covered in blood. Patrick.

'Trish, what happened? Listen I've got a shawl somewhere. I know I have. It was so cold in the airport I had to muffle myself up in it.'

Miranda heard herself rabbiting on about airports and stopovers and hot and cold as she found the shawl, wrapped Trish up more warmly, and attended to their travel kettle. How lovely Trish looked, sitting muffled up in the bed, her enormous brown eyes startled in her pale face. She wrapped her slender brown fingers gratefully round the plastic mug Miranda had given her. 'I'm so cold, so cold Miranda.'

'Trish', she sat down and put her arms firmly around her shaken friend 'What has happened?'

'He's not breathing I tell you. We must get to him.'

'Jim's taking care of him, Trish. He'll be OK with Jim. Just drink your tea and get warm. You're in shock you know.'

'No. I must go to him.'

'Well, we'll both go. But keep that blanket round you. And drink the tea.' Miranda suddenly thought of the mini-bar, so far scrupulously untouched. 'Here, I'm putting a brandy in. Just get it down you and we'll go next door.'

She grabbed one of the small bottles from the fridge at random, wrestled the top off, and poured it in the tea. Trish swallowed it down almost in one, without comment or choking, without reacting to it at all. Miranda was tempted to try and offer her another, but Trish was already heading for the door, trailing her blanket behind her. They stepped out into the hot sticky air, and Miranda was startled at the power of shock that could so powerfully overcome the heat of a night on the Equator.

Jassie and Wolfie were there. Jim must have phoned them. They filled up Patrick and Trish's chalet. Wolfie was on the phone, urgent, rousing his remaining boat staff. Jassie was rushing backwards and forwards from the bathroom. There was a heap of stained towels in the corner. Jim had had the same thought she had and was ransacking the mini bar for comforters for all. They all grabbed one of the little bottles he offered them and gulped it down. Even Miranda.

It was certainly helping to warm Trish up, her shivering had nearly stopped. Miranda quickly went over and turned the air con and fan off. The room would be stiflingly warm in no time and keep Trish safe. But where was Patrick? Was he out there in the water somewhere? Miranda settled Trish on the bed, wrapping their bedspread around her too.

'Go to Pat, Go to Pat.' She kept urging. Miranda followed Jassie into the bathroom.

Jim was kneeling over Patrick, who was lying on the marbled floor. There were a lot of reddened towels around his head. Miranda took one horrified look and stared questioningly at Jim. They had both heard an evening of bitter quarrels, but it was impossible to believe that Trish, of all people could have… How truly dreadful if it had come to this. Not Patrick and Trish. No.

And she did love him so much. That was as clear now to Miranda as it had been in her dream. Miranda looked her horrified question at Jim. Who shook his head. And picked up a coconut that was lying on the bathroom floor. 'And the coconut survived' he said, turning the unbroken fruit over and over, thoughtfully. That should have been Patrick's line. To her shame, Miranda burst into tears.

The coconut told the story. The Shoal was used to hearing the ominous rustling and crackling in the tops of tall palms, and then wincing as they heard the careless crash of the descending coconut. As on all the islands, the coconut palms were carefully corralled and coppiced, but this one had somehow found its way through the half bathroom roof, like a guided missile aimed at Patrick's head. It wasn't the force of the blow, the coconut itself, but it had knocked him off balance and he had fallen against the marbled edge of the basin. Hard.

The gash to his head had a nasty flat look to it, when it wasn't welling with blood that Jassie was trying to wipe away. Poor Trish had had a nightmare awakening. The double crash and the silence. And no Patrick in the bed beside her.

'Get me another towel Miranda. I've used all the ice out of this fridge, go and get yours.' Jassie's authority was as re-assuring as Jim's, and Miranda was able to set herself on automatic pilot and do as she was told. It had suddenly occurred to her that this was just the sort of thing Carmen M would do. Had she been here? Did she lurk in bathrooms, endlessly whitening those terrible teeth? After all, in Hollywood movies nowadays, women regularly beat men to a pulp. An image of Patrick's head came vividly to mind as she thought the word 'pulp'. Why did the world want women to be as violent as some men?

Why was the world in love with violence? It was frightening and sordid. It led to the sickening flatness of Patrick's head. Miranda thought of the stained towels and bed linen. How much blood had Patrick lost?

Then suddenly Ali and Elder Mo were in the chalet too, and it became very crowded. Miranda tried to coax Trish back to their chalet, but she wouldn't leave Patrick. Miranda couldn't blame her. She knew how she would feel if it was Jim lying there, reddening all the towels that could be found. She certainly wouldn't have left him. What was wrong? What was happening to them? Something had got into this dive trip. Some small something that was making it all go horribly wrong. But what? It was liked being trapped in a nightmare, unable to wake up properly. Perhaps not till Gordo arrived…

She wanted to ask Jim, but he looked pale and shaken. Jim! I could kick that horrible coconut all over the island, thought Miranda grimly.

So that was her Carmen Miranda moment – at last.

Wolfie had brought a stretcher over from the Medical Centre and he, Jim and Samir had stretchered Patrick over there. Jassie was with him now. At least Inga had plenty of company tonight. They had decided not to wake the rest of the party. And had also decided that, come morning, as soon as it was light enough, if they still had no communications, they would attempt to get Patrick off the island on the dive boat and motor to the Staff Island. There they might be able to make some contact with the doctor. Or even find a seaplane.

The remnant of the Shoal waved sadly from the jetty as Patrick was loaded aboard the dive boat. Miranda was impressed they had such a hi-tech stretcher on the island. He was all strapped up and held in – cocooned from the effects of the waves. Though the sea round the little island was as calm as ever and surely the storm that had been rocking the outer reefs would be dying down now. All they had to do was get Patrick safely to the Staff Island where a plane could land.

What a terrible and blackly comic thing to happen. To Patrick of all people. The doyen of toilet humour. Poor Trish. She was as ashen as he was. Wolfie and Jassie and Elder Mo were going with them. If the sea wouldn't let them get to the Staff Island, there was an Italian Resort Island, about five hours away. There might be communications there. And there was a seaplane. And almost certainly a doctor, as that was where Oz, the flying doctor, usually lived.

Jim, Todd, Mal and Miranda waved them off sadly. Samir was nowhere to be seen, so presumably he was still with an imprisoned Inga. Ali hadn't appeared but as they were now out of eggs, and apparently all breakfast stuffs apart from the cereals that lived permanently on the buffet, there really wasn't much point. The usual tray of chapattis had appeared though, together with yogurt. But Miranda, after watching Todd drown his chapattis in bright red ketchup, had just had a cup of black tea. She suddenly wondered why they all hadn't piled on to the boat and gone with Wolfie and his crew. After all, they were to leave this island late afternoon as it was. Patrick couldn't wait. She understood that. But why hadn't they gone?

Sensibly she told herself there was no point. The boat was sailing away from the airport and the storm clouds. It was the helicopter that would take them to their plane tonight. If they went to the airport by boat, they would have to add another week to their holiday. Nevertheless, Miranda knew that she wished they had left the small island. And not looked back.

Mal and Jim had breakfasted on beers they had helped themselves to from the bar. Scrupulously leaving their room numbers on the bar receipts Miranda was glad to see. Things hadn't completely broken down. Yet. They ate nothing. Apart from Todd with his blood red breads. And Miranda took all the uneaten chapattis from the table. Still they were wasting stuff.

The usual boiling of fish hung around the jetty, immune to the tragedies going on above. No doubt they had enough tragedy of their own in their underwater world. Miranda began mechanically to make the leftover breakfast into the little bread balls that she scattered every morning so that even the tiniest fish would get a chance to eat.

But first she threw in one large piece whole to let them know that feeding was to start. A little striper swam round the bread and finally darted bravely at it, taking a tiny bit and hurtling away. The chapatti didn't appear to put up any resistance, so the next striper came in. Another bite. The bread, saintly and forgiving, floated harmlessly round without retaliating, and within seconds was the centre of a frenzy of fish of all sorts and colours. Tiny stripers contending valiantly with enormous parrot fish and getting away with a crumb here and there. There was something disturbing about it, but Miranda didn't want to follow that train of thought.

They would miss their usual breakfast toasts and rolls this morning. And why did they like toast, she wondered, trying to distract herself. Why did they like bread at all? Was she being fair letting them get so confident with a member of the human species? Just where did they get those fish for the evening buffets after all? We don't do any good by coming here thought Miranda. Not for the first time.

But, but, but ... it was impossible. She and Jim had talked this through so many times. The situation on earth appeared to be a problem they could not solve. However surely they should, and could, strive not to make it any worse? Anyway, whatever it might or might not have done to the island, it hadn't done them much good coming here this time, had it?

But there was another more immediate problem to be faced. Tomorrow was the last day of their holiday. And there were no guarantees that anyone would come for them. And as for the chance of making contact with the outside world with Wolfie and Jassie gone ... They were supposed to be back mid-afternoon though. In time to take the remnant of the Shoal to the sand spit where their helicopter would land, and take them back to the main island. Airport Island. If there was still a world out there. If the raging storms would stop for an hour or two. But it seemed that, as soon as the boat had left the reef, the waves had gathered their strength again and began to rock the island. Miranda could only hope that Patrick's boat was sailing into calmer waters. He was in enough trouble as it was.

She consoled herself with the memory of his hi-tech stretcher. Hopefully, he was locked safely in stasis. And what were Jim and Mal and Todd and she herself going to do? As they were scheduled to leave for their plane tomorrow morning, no-one would be diving today. And they couldn't search for the lost snorkelers as they had neither the dive boat nor the boat that was last seen containing Mo the Boathook.

Miranda's wanderings had carried her along to the main jetty, and she found she was staring at a heron. He was standing on one foot, posed by a rock-pool. They looked at each other for a bit, until Miranda retreated. The poor thing probably wouldn't have much time for peaceful fishing now that the small island had been opened to tourists. Miranda crept along the edge of the island, pushing between the mangroves and the waves, away from the fishing area, thinking that if she were a fish, she would be longing for someone to come along who had the power and authority to chase that fierce fisher away.

And now her footprints had spoiled the lovely morning beach too! It had been such a perfect sweep of polished smoothness. She had never felt such soft fine sand under her feet. It was like the fluff of chickens, the downy fur of baby animals, the finest wool carpet in the world. The sun fluoresced on the white plastic beach chairs – two to a villa – until even they became beautiful.

But Miranda was not the only one to have spoilt the morning beach. Someone had been here before she had, before the heron had, perhaps even before the fish of the morning had freed themselves sleepily from their coral cocoons. Because here were rather a lot of footprints, hurrying and rushing together down to the water. Down to an odd shaped – or was that boat shaped? – scrape in the sand. She remembered the fruitless search for Young Mo and went to get Mal and Jim.

They stood silent, staring at the footprints in the sand. Todd had joined them. The waves stayed back, as if wanting them to miss nothing. The boat had clearly come ashore at the small beach at the back here, with its little rotting wooden pier. And footsteps in the sand suggested that the rest of the staff had been waiting for it. The hurrying feet stopped at the boat and then nothing.

They had all quietly left. With Mo the Boathook. He must have hung about till morning somewhere offshore and come back for them. After breakfast. Because they had been served a cooked breakfast, albeit a somewhat sparse one, in the dining hall. Someone had made chapattis and tea, at any rate. And someone had cleaned and cleared Jim and Miranda's chalet, eradicating all signs of the night's trauma. He wouldn't have come back for the staff till it was light, because of the taboo.

And yet, up to Inga's accident, he had seemed happy enough to live and work on Small Island. They all had. Miranda remembered their relaxed sleep on the quiet dive boat. Jim and the remainder of his Shoal stood for a long time watching the footsteps that went one way only. Jim, Miranda, Mal and Todd. Now we are four, thought Miranda. She felt sick.

Then she remembered Inga. Locked in her pod. Inga and Samir? Yes, she must still be there. He wouldn't leave her. So there were still six of them, alone on Small Island. And in a few hours their helicopter would come. If the storms held off for long enough. Just one more night to get through.

But it wouldn't come to the island. It would land on that little spit of sand somewhere off on the horizon. And how were they to get there if Wolfie and Jassie didn't come back with the boat? People would laugh if she said that she was terrified at the idea of having to stay here – trapped on Small Island. Trapped in Paradise. Surely she couldn't be wanting to get back to work?

But Miranda found that she did. Very much. The hot, dusty Company Town, where everything was so ordinary and organized and people didn't go to the pool one minute and disappear the next seemed like Paradise now. She could almost envy Patrick and Trish. They were being flown back to that world. Like the others, they had vanished from the island.

They had lunched at the bar. There was water still. Plenty of beer. And Miranda had found bread, cheese and pizza toppings in the large fridge, and had manufactured a sort of sandwich lunch. They had sat for a long time, staring out to sea. Picking at the coconut and bananas Miranda

113

had cut up for them. And drinking beer after beer. They seemed to have forgotten about the room numbers, and she was worriedly trying to keep count of what they had taken. She didn't think Small Island could afford to give them free drinks. Especially not after a week like this one. Not a single new diver had arrived, and they had been disappearing as fast as a shoal of North Sea codfish.

'We must go and see Inga.'

'And Samir.'

'Yes, he won't have gone.'

They all took turns at saying that, at regular intervals, except for Todd, but no-one made to leave the sunset bar. Sometimes they wondered if Wolfie and Jassie had found the doctor at the Italian Island, or if they were still out there. Searching. Nobody directly mentioned Patrick anymore. The blood seeping through his bandages as he was stretchered on to the boat was vivid enough in all their thoughts. They couldn't even talk about Diane and Alison.

'There's a little boat over there. Remember?' They all looked puzzled.

'What are you talking about, Jim?' Mel opened another bottle of beer, and offered it round.

'Thanks. I mean on the sand spit where the helicopter landed. There was a small boat there. I noticed, because I was wondering just what would happen if they left you there and no boat came.'

So she hadn't been alone with her worries, thought Miranda triumphantly. She hadn't been the only one wondering about that, about being stranded on that tiny bit of sand. Although Jim had found a practical solution. 'Jim! What do you mean?' She suddenly realized the implications of what he was saying.

She tried to think back to the helicopter landing. It was hard to remember. They had been a different Shoal then, waiting sunnily on that sandbank for their Small Island holiday to start. Was there really a boat there, or was it wishful thinking on Jim's part?

'I'm going to get it. I'll windsurf out there. Then we can be sure to get off the island tomorrow and be on that landing spit when our helicopter arrives.

'I'll come with you, Jim.' That was Mal. Obviously relieved to have the prospect of doing something. Todd lit up another cigarette and looked cynical. Which he always did very well.

'No. You stay here. It wouldn't hurt to have another look for the girls. Just in case.'

Jim always believed that the best place to search for a missing person, a missing animal, a missing object, was in the place that they were last seen. Once, when Chessman had gone missing for two whole days, Jim had persistently kept searching in the desert scrub right behind their house, where Miranda had last seen him chasing lizards. And, eventually, they had heard him. And found the collapsed, abandoned section of pipeline with an angry and dehydrated Chess stuffed into it.

'Jim. You take Mal with you. Please. Todd is here. And I'll go and see Inga and Samir. I'll wait there till you get back.' She could sit in the clinic by herself if necessary. But Jim, never one to hang about, was already hoisting himself up on to one of the surfers with smooth efficiency.

'It's going to be dark soon enough. I've got to get there and back. And, listen Miranda, if it takes longer than I thought I won't make it back till morning. I won't risk a night crossing. You can all wait up in the sunset bar. Is that OK, Mal?' Mal was fine with that. He seemed to understand that Jim didn't want Miranda to be alone, especially not at night.

'Take some water, Jim. At least.'

Miranda handed him a bottle from the bar fridge. And, quite suddenly, he was gone; scudding confidently across the lagoon, heading for the channel and the open sea, hurtling towards the little sand bar they had landed on in some other lifetime, a week ago. Miranda turned away from Todd and Mal. Her eyes had suddenly filled with tears. We didn't even kiss goodbye. But it wasn't goodbye. He'll be back in an hour

115

or so. After all, he wasn't … But the thought didn't complete. She couldn't make sense of it.

After a while Jim was a dot on the water, and then he was swallowed up by the waves. No, thought Miranda hastily, swallowed up by perspective. Not the waves. It was quite a long way to that little landing strip. She felt sick at the thought that Jim would hardly be likely to make it back tonight, whatever he had said. She couldn't even wish him to try. She didn't want him out on the vast ocean. Alone. At night. Surrounded by wild waves and with no island man to tell him what was safe.

Todd had started on the whisky now. He seemed set on drinking the island dry.

He and Mal talked a bit. They kicked Jim's idea about. Agreed it was a good one. It would be terrible to see the helicopter land, to see it sitting there, and just to watch it fly away. 'And to be left on Small Island with …' Miranda didn't say it though, as she didn't know how to complete the sentence.

'It'll be fine, Miranda. Don't look so worried. It isn't that far. He'll likely be back here before it's dark.' Miranda appreciated Mal's attempts to comfort her. They didn't help, but she was grateful that he tried. Todd said nothing. And the sun continued to sink towards the cloud filled horizon. Todd and Mal talked quietly to each other. Mainly about work. They worked in the same company department. It was all computer chat and soothingly boring, although it left Miranda a bit too free to think her own thoughts. Come on now, she chided herself, if I were Carmen what would I be doing? Kicking someone's backside, came the dreary answer. And what use is that? I suppose uber-me would have sailed off into the wide blue yonder to rescue these hopeless pathetic guys.

Nobody ever rescued Carmen. She was a *Gal Who Can Take of Herself.* She was a survivor. And she didn't have arthritic knees. But there again, thought Miranda, I am still here, aren't I? Surely the day hadn't come when she was going to have to admit to having something in common with her appalling heroine? But if she was going to think like that then she was acknowledging to herself that something had happened, something was happening. They were being … She made a hasty return to Carmen.

Now, if Carmen were left on an island with two guys – two good looking guys too, she thought, looking at Mal and Todd … If Carmen Miranda were with them, let's face it, they wouldn't be talking to each other about computers. They would be … well, it didn't actually bear thinking about what they might be doing if this was being filmed. Think of something else, Miranda. Quickly.

'Want another one, Miranda?'

How many Banana Mananas have I drunk? It's a good thing they weren't alcoholic. They were quite filling too. Which was another good thing, as there wasn't any food left in that fridge. There was a bunch of green bananas ripening on the bar, coconuts on the tallest palms. And one shoal of tame fish in the lagoon. And I reckon that is about it, thought Miranda to herself. Anyway, even if they were starving, it would be very mean to fish the tame shoal in the lagoon. There will be supplies somewhere in the centre of the island, where the kitchens are. But … Once again, she couldn't complete the sentence.

'I'm outta here.' Todd stood up abruptly. Steady on his feet, she noticed. His voice was clear, his hands weren't shaking. He had the last whisky bottle from the bar with him. 'Gotta party.'

Party? Miranda realized that it was already late afternoon. The sun was strong, the sea was bright, but the shadows were sharp – warning that the tropical night would come quickly. Mal watched Todd go. He didn't look pleased.

'We've got about an hour's daylight left at most, Miranda. I wonder …'

He put down his glass. He had been drinking beer and the empty bottles had piled up beside him. He too seemed steady on his feet, his voice unblurred. But he had had a lot too. 'I could just about windsurf round the island in twenty minutes. Easy.'

'Mal!' Have you gone mad?

'It's OK. I have to do something. I'll just go round once. You wait for me here. It'll relax me. I'm never going to sleep otherwise.'

He had been scanning the horizon anxiously for signs of Jim and the boat, as had Miranda. But there was nothing but the sea, the path of the sinking sun, and the white breakers. And now he wanted to do one more sweep for the missing snorkelers, hoping to find who knows what?

'We can both sleep in the bar by the way Miranda, if you want. If Jim doesn't … If Jim has to spend the night on the sand bar.'

But Mal, Miranda wanted to say, Mal, when I swam out to the giggling girls I did see something. I know I said I didn't, but I forgot. Till Gordo reminded me in my dreams that night. She had seen wavering fingers of green flowing through the water. Way below me. Wavering fingers of green, Mal.

What colour is blood underwater?

But she couldn't say it. She could remember it in the dream. Vividly. Those green ribbon arms. But had her memory of events on the reef been altered by the dream?

What had she seen that day? What she said was, 'Where did Todd go?' If Mal could wait till Todd came back. If they went together … but that was no good either. Diane and Alison had been together.

'Todd?' Mal's voice was as sharp as when he questioned Miranda about what she had seen, what she had heard. 'He's got an invite to meet Mr Al-Auddin, or at any rate his stewardesses. We won't see him again till after the party.'

Well. If a Siren wanted to lure Todd, she could hardly find a better bait. That's for sure. Even Carmen wouldn't prove quite as tempting as that. Although, she would be just about Todd's type. Miranda thought of Carmen, dressed in her white thong bikini, wriggling temptingly on the end of a line. Yes, Todd would certainly get his bottom kicked under those circumstances. Surely neither Todd nor Mal really believed that there was anyone in the locked and shuttered palace of Al-Auddin. And if there was, how could they get through those thorny gates?

Mal was in the sea now, about to get up on the windsurfer and head for the channel to the ocean. Miranda knew why he wanted to go round and round the island. Just in case … Just in case there was something, some little clue left by Diane that no-one had noticed. After all, others had conducted the sea search. Wolfie and Jassie in the large boat, Mo the Boathook in the smaller. Mal had only searched the beach. And then Patrick's accident had distracted them. He just wanted to be sure that they had missed nothing of Diane's. Something that perhaps only the eye of love would see. Alison seemed to be peripheral to the search now, as she had been when she was present.

It's all too sad. Miranda's eyes were stinging with water as salty as the lagoon's. And she must stop Mal. They didn't need any more sadness. She waded into the lagoon after him. She knew what she wanted to say. She wanted to say: Shouldn't we all stick together, Mal? Think about it. Think about what's happening. We are disappearing, one by one. There is only you, me and Todd left. And Inga?

But we haven't seen her, have we? We haven't visited her today. If the few remaining staff – the skeletons – took their chance and legged it with Mo the Boathook, how do we know she's still here? If only the sea hadn't flushed those footprints away. Because she would like to go back and check for Inga's long, slender feet. She would like to count, to see if they all did leave, or if there is someone left here with them.

What if Inga and Samir had gone? They could already be on the home archipelago, safe and cosy with Samir's family. And what if, when she counted the feet, one set of footprints was missing? And that, somewhere, on the island, keeping himself hidden from them was … who? Ali? One of the Mo's? And what if there were extra footprints – feet that they never knew had been here?

What made them go just then? Why? They were running. Did she really want to know?

'Mal. Mal …' Mal was up and ready to go.

'I'm just going round the island, Miranda. I'll be back, right here at the channel in half an hour or so. Before sunset. Get me a drink in, if you can find anything!' He was impatient. Irritated with her obvious wish to stop him. Mal. She wanted to warn him. Just don't go. But what could she say? How could she say it? When she didn't even know what 'it' was?

Anyway he was up. And then he was off, towards the reef edge. The wind was perfect. It fairly scudded him along. Miranda watched him and quickly turned and began to wade back to the shore. The tide seemed to be coming in again. Fast. She was going to leave the beach now. Right now. When Mal called out to her – and he would call out to her, his voice full of laughter and fun, she would not be there to hear him. She would resist the siren call. After all, she did warn him.

Only, Miranda, you didn't warn him. Did you? Carmen would have. No she wouldn't though. Carmen and her ilk only had a few words, most of them vile. And anyway how could this be conveyed in words? She hadn't even put it into words in her own head yet. She didn't want to admit what she knew. She didn't even know if she knew 'it'. She thought she knew it in her dreams. But they faded and she couldn't hang on to them. It rustled the mangroves, although Gordo wasn't there. It banged and clattered on their doors in the middle of the nights. But they were all so tired, from traveling or diving, or the heat.

The dreams told her. But then she forgot them. And now she couldn't be sure what was dream and what wasn't. So how could she make Mal believe it? When she couldn't yet believe it herself. Goodbye Mal. Wherever Diane is, that is where you will soon be.

A perfect black triangle appeared in the crest of a tiny wave and a small shark flashed past Miranda, hunting right in the shallows, where the hot salt stung Miranda's scratched and reddened ankles. She waded quickly out of the water, intending to walk into the heart of the island, as if there was safety there. But she stopped at the edge of mangroves. The implications of something Mal had said suddenly arrived at the emergency centre of her brain. She was heading towards Aladdin's palace. And Mal had said that was where Todd was going. But … he had said there was a party. So he must have had an invitation. Something.

But would she really find a party going on there. And the whole Shoal dancing merrily away, just waiting for Miranda to turn up. Miranda the Party Girl! Now that was a joke if there ever was one. It wasn't some horrible surprise party for something or other? Miranda checked hastily through her mental calendar. It certainly wasn't her birthday, and it wasn't Jim's. And anyway, she and Jim didn't really celebrate such things. Never mind surprise parties. It wasn't their wedding anniversary. But who knows what the Shoal might be celebrating.

She called in at their villa. She had better do something with herself. Shower. Change. Just in case there was a party. At least there was still plenty of hot water. And no. She mustn't think of Jim – as if he too had really vanished from the island. As if he was not waiting for her at the villa of Aladdin with a party hat on.

She looked at herself in the mirror. Her face was completely white – strangely white for the tropics. They have stolen the loveliness of middle-age, thought Miranda, but they have left the sad part. Because now when she looked at herself in mirrors, it was the faces of the dead that stared back at her. There was her mother, her granny. And, sometimes, a glimpse of her father. His worried look. And why was she so white and worried if she was going off to a party?

She had better put some extra mortar on then, said Miranda to her mirror self, as she busily plastered away at the cracks. Although it would all be melted off in no time in the equatorial night and the horrible truth would be revealed. It was fine for Carmen, who had her team of beauticians and hairdressers with her at all times – and she was only ever seen in her best-profile mode anyway. Miranda locked the door carefully behind her and made for the interior of the island.

Oh, those thorns. Why didn't they ever find that other entrance to the palace? If Todd's in there he must have found it. If she could find the entrance to the clinic, then she could see if Inga was still there. It would surely be safe for her to come out now. Could this small island ever be safe?

Things grew so fast in the tropics. She had never appreciated how hard these island gardeners worked. Miranda looked puzzled at the path. Where was the palace? Where was the little notice signalling the clinic opposite? There were thorns aplenty. A golden insect about the size of a humming bird whirred past with its fingers in its ears. Wait a minute. Could cockroaches fly with their fingers in their ears? Perhaps she had gone through the looking glass. Did cockroaches have ears? Did they have fingers? And why would they block up their ears anyway?

Unless … Todd! He was the only reason why anyone on Small Island would have their fingers to their ears. Miranda always had to keep her 'delete' button on standby during the Todd tirades. He must still be here. And he must be on the beach. That's where my bathroom friend was fleeing from. He must have decided against the party. Things really were bad though if Todd had turned down an invite to a party with blonde air hostesses. Your grammar is really going to pot under all this stress Miranda, she lectured herself. From where my bathroom friend was fleeing would be better.

She was not alone on the island then. Todd was still here. Why did it have to be Todd that was left? Probably that is just what he was thinking. Miranda laughed in a hysterical way. Middle-aged Miranda would surely be the last person he would choose to be alone on a desert island with. You're doing it again, Miranda, using a preposition to end a sentence with. Alone with on a desert island, she corrected herself sternly. At least keep your grammar together, even if everything else is all over the place.

Them being alone here together might even drive him over the edge, which might just be what you intended ... but she couldn't as yet name their attacker. Even to herself. She could run away from Todd or go to him. Follow the cockroach or go to Todd. And she thought that ... her mind once again refused a name it, Something small, intended that they should meet. So they might as well get it over with. She turned back. After all, they couldn't avoid each other for long on Small Island.

Todd and Miranda stood in silence as the tide swallowed up the tiny beach. Whatever Todd had been ranting about before, he had now got it out of his system. What was there to say anyway?

What desert island discs should we choose, Todd and I? *Hit the Road Jack and Don't you Come Back No More*? *The Party's Over*? There are no surprise parties on this island. But plenty of surprises. Todd was staring at something the incoming tide had brought to the edge of the white sand beach. It was a piece of wood. It had the word *SLAND* on it. It's not just a piece of any old wood Miranda, the waves sang. Look closely. This is a piece of boat. A piece of boat come back to its island to die.

No, thought Miranda. No. No. No. This could come from any island. And it looks like it has been in the water some time. She was not even going to try and think what that boat on the sand spit looked like. She never even saw it. But there was no way it had come from that boat.

At that moment, the windsurfer – a horse without its rider – galloped crazily past the channel. Caught in the current it was whirling, oddly fast, round and round the small island. Sometimes it was upright, sometimes it lay flat against the waves.

Mal ... Why hadn't she told him?

Told him what, Miranda, murmured the waves soothingly. Told him what?

Did this mean that she and Todd were last two people on the island? Perhaps they were the last two people in the world. If so, thought Miranda, the human race is going to die out. Ought they to be staring suspiciously at each other, wondering who did this. But who did what? That was the question. And to who? And to whom, Miranda. And to whom?

One by one they had been disposed of. Until there were just the two of them left. Were they supposed to fight and kill each other a la Christie? There were no bodies. Except Inga, Miranda thought with a start. Was it only yesterday that she and Jim had hopped up the thorny path … the path to the castle where the princess lay in her enchanted sleep? But Inga was alive. We saw her. And Samir. So there were four of them on the island. Unless …

Inga. The blonde princess sleeping amongst the thorns. Except that Miranda had seen no path to the clinic, no sign for the clinic. Had she even seen the gates of Aladdin's palace? Or just a mass of thorns?

No. She was not going to worry about that. She couldn't worry about Jim, couldn't admit what there was to worry about. And Wolfie, Mo and Jassie? They were fine. She knew it. So a bit of board broke off somebody's boat, so what? They would all soon be back. It might not have been a Small Island boat anyway. Many many boats must have come to grief around these islands.

There was a glorious sunset going on. Miranda hoped Jim was remembering to look. She hoped they all were, on their various islands. Soon it would be dark. But she mustn't even think about the coming night. Would she have to spend it alone on the island with Todd? He had been quite silent, standing beside her, staring at the bit of boat. Whatever outburst had startled the Bathroom Cockroach had been quickly over.

'Todd. It might not be …' She wanted to say it might not be a Small Island boat at all, but couldn't. Fearful of what he would come back with.

Todd threw down his cigarette. 'That's it then. The hell with it. I'm going to party.' He followed that up with a load of expletives about the trip, as he leapt over the undefended bar, and began to pile up bottles of whisky.

'Todd?' Miranda didn't even know what to ask him. Todd, what about Inga? Todd, what is happening? Todd, you aren't going to leave me, are you? Todd are you going to drink yourself into oblivion?

'Todd, what's Inga doing?' was what came out of her mouth.

'Well, not much, if she's in the hyperbaric chamber.' Todd laughed. It was quite chilling.

'But Todd, what's happening here?'

'Oh, Miranda.' He had never used her name before, or even looked at her directly before. Things really were serious.

'What's happening?' He mimicked her.

'Todd. Just tell me. Do you know what's happening?' Miranda suddenly found she couldn't care less about what Todd thought. If he would only put it into words, perhaps she could too.

'Well, yes, Miranda, I surely do.' He put on a mock-Southern accent 'Aaah am going to get drunk with those lovely blonde stewardesses that Aladdin guy keeps in that little house of his. If I'm going next, I'm going to go happy.'

Todd, what do you mean *going next*? Todd, don't leave me. Miranda silently watched as he made his way back into the centre of Small Island, clutching several whisky bottles. He was already unsteady on his feet.

She knew exactly how he would have answered her anyway. What do I mean? You know what I mean, Miranda. You know exactly what I mean. Maybe he had known when he first caught sight of Small Island from their sand bar. Todd was at home with death. He knew they were all dead men walking. And he refused to care. He had deliberately turned his back on life – endorsed the choice our first parents made for us so long ago. But he would never forgive. And never forget.

The woman whom you gave to be with me, she gave me fruit from the tree and so I ate.

It's all your fault, Miranda. Everything is your fault. You and all your kind. The least you could do is be young, glamorous, sexy. Available.

Have big boobs. But, no, most of you can't even manage that, can you? As she feared. Carmen was his ideal woman. To be with Todd was to be more lonely than to be on her own. She would let him go. Just as if she had a choice in the matter.

But she was not on her own anyway. She was on an island. With staff. They never counted footsteps. There could still be staff. Inga and Samir would be in the chamber just along the path there. Samir wouldn't have left Inga. He wouldn't have finally checked her out of the chamber without a doctor's say so. He loved her.

And Jim and Wolfie and Jassie were heading back to the island at full tilt in their various boats. With the snorkelers. And all the Mo's with them. And Todd was partying away with the whole of Mr Al-Auddin's harem. So Small Island was really quite crowded. Even Chessman was there somewhere, busily rustling the bushes around her.

And Carmen? Miranda hadn't seen her for a while. So it was her that was gone and lost for good. Perhaps it was her and Al Nino who set off in that boat. Miranda remembered the rushing footprints in the white sand. Or maybe Mr Al-Auddin had invited her to his party. Good riddance to bad rubbish.

So she would go back to her chalet and go to sleep. And when she woke up Jim would be there sleeping beside her, as he always was. There was no question about it. Nothing else was possible. Jim must be fine. He was on his way back. She would leave their chalet light on, to guide him. So he wouldn't open the door in darkness.

She unlocked the door of the villa, and stopped to look out into the island night. For one last time? Clouds muffled the moon and stars. It would be a night of soaking rain. Although it was still stiflingly hot. For the moment there was silence. The lull before the storm? The waves were close. And their sound was oddly comforting. Because otherwise the island was quiet. And dark. Chessman had fallen asleep somewhere, in mid-purr, on a nest of leaves. Nothing rustled. Even the Dalek lights seemed to have packed up and left. The one outside their villa still gleamed, but she couldn't see that any of the others had come on. Thank goodness that one was still up and running – a signal to help Jim back.

The thought: *Or a signal to something else* tried to get into Miranda's worry list and failed. She was keeping it packed full. No room for any more. No room even for something small.

Miranda shut the door quickly. She didn't want to have to notice what was happening to the other villas. The empty ones. If she had any spare worry space left, she thought hysterically to herself, then she might have been getting a bit upset that she seemed to be completely alone on the island and those thorns were … but she was not completely alone. She was not. There was Todd. For what comfort that thought was. And hadn't she heard something as she ran back in and slammed the door closed? Had there been a noise, coming from the dark heart of the island? A jangling, dancing noise. And was the scent of a strange perfume once again overcoming the frangipani fragrance?

Well, thought Miranda, tucking herself up in bed. She didn't know and she didn't care. Because she was going to sleep. She was not alone. Of course not. Everyone had gone to bed early. And she would follow their example. And, when she woke up, Jim would be there. Resolutely she got into bed, to face what was sure to be the longest night of her life. She would keep all the lights in the room on and just read. She wouldn't close her eyes for a moment. She couldn't face those dreams. Not with no Jim to wake up to. Anyway, there was no point in trying to sleep yet, as he would be coming through that door at any moment. She was not alone. She was not alone. To spend a night alone on Small Island was unthinkable.

If she went to sleep, that would certainly be it. Full stop. The world would end there and then. Nonsense, Miranda, she told herself, you are talking nonsense. But, if by any chance she did fall asleep before Jim arrived, she would not wake up in the night. Not once, Miranda told her subconscious firmly. She would have no need to go to the loo. After all, she had gone rather short on water today. She should be safely dehydrated, and would not meet the Bathroom Cockroach till the morning.

She turned hastily to Fifties London with Janet Frame. Who had now left her Southland Island and begun some heroic traveling. It was all so reassuringly grey and rainy. Miranda even smiled, reading of Frame's disappointment at visiting the actual places that were named so grandly as Marble Arch, The Elephant and Castle, Piccadilly Circus. She could remember similar disappointments from her own childhood.

They had been driving to her granny's house, through a grey and rainy Manchester when she had seen the sign. FREE HOUSE.

Free House!

Miranda knew how expensive houses were. Her parents had been looking and looking for somewhere to live, and now they had found something. And they were going to her granny's to ask if she could lend them some money to put down. They would have to put a lot of money on to this house they were going to buy. Dad had to keep his job. That was the thing. It would be alright if he could keep his job. The house had a small attic bedroom for Miranda, overlooking the tiny garden at the back, with its towering holly tree. It was 'the best we could hope for'. They would have to sell the car. If anyone could be found to buy an old Riley, with its back doors tied on with string.

And now, right in front of them, was a free house! A big house too, with a pub attached, and the grown-ups were too busy talking to notice. She must try to tell them, to attract their attention. But the wall of thorns between the back and front seat of the car was going to tear her to pieces.

How could she get to her parents to let them know? To tell them there was this house, an enormous house near to Granny, going free. It almost certainly had a big garden too. Maybe a garden as wonderful as her grandmother's!

She must find a way. If only they would stop talking for a moment they must see it. How could they not see it? Grown-ups went around with their eyes shut. It had such a bright, glowing sign too. Miranda wiped at the steamy back window to see it clearer.

THE GOLDEN COCKROACH.

Her parents went on with their worried chatter. But the fat insect on the sign winked at Miranda. And admonished her, in large bold letters to: TAKE COURAGE. TAKE COURAGE.

THE LAST DAY

Their last day. This was the day that a boat would take them to the sand spit landing strip, and from the far horizon a dot of a helicopter would grow and grow, until it was big enough to fly them all the way back to the real world. Or was that supposed to have happened yesterday? Miranda found she could no longer remember what day of the week it was. But she had to fight hard to stop the words: My Last Day coming into her mind. Her worry list was full. Full. So she would just keep it that way. Then she wouldn't be able to fit any more worries in.

For all her horror of the night, she had slept right through. She had woken up suddenly to find the room filled with sunshine, and her Janet Frame crumpled underneath her. She could remember no dreams, no midnight trips to the loo. Nothing but blackness and blankness. Well, Gordo must have given up knocking at her dream door now and would have long since returned to the shores of his distant expat homeland with a planeload of disappointed German divers. He would be furious that he had missed one of Jim's famous trips. But why hadn't something else knocked at her door, rustled at her from the mangroves, splashed up to the very walls of the villa?

If it had, Miranda hadn't heard it. She didn't wake till a low buzzing woke her. Turning to find Jim's alarm clock and silence it, Miranda found the Bathroom Cockroach whirring off from beside her, just as if it had spent the night on Jim's pillow.

Bright sunlight filled every corner of the room. And there was no Jim. No Jim anywhere. And how could life go on if there was no Jim. Who would organize it? What would be the point of organizing it anymore?

Miranda laughed hysterically. What a good thing she kept such a full worry list. With so many things to catch up on. Because otherwise, she might simply go mad, as she seemed to be on a tiny island, in the middle of nowhere. The outer edge of nowhere, in fact. Alone. No, Miranda. Don't think about that. Think about Inga and Samir instead. Again, she tried not to remember slender footprints, hurrying through white sand.

And who was to say that Wolfie and Jassie weren't back, with news of everyone? Or perhaps the manager and full complement of staff had arrived today from wherever it was they had been stranded? She would simply go outside and see what was happening. She would do it right now. If you don't jump off the high dive board straight away, you don't jump at all. She stepped quickly out into the Paradise world outside before she could change her mind.

Small Island had been washed by a night of rain. How wonderful she had slept through all the clatter. Miraculous really, given the way she hadn't been sleeping. Because if the rain, beating at the door, had woken her, she might have been pulled out into the night, against her better wishes, and … Did she have faint memories of a quiet and soothing whirring lulling her back to sleep during the stormy night?

The lagoon burst with waves. So the storm was still raging out there. OK. That was why they weren't back yet. It was as simple as that. They couldn't make it. Nothing had happened to them. And they would send someone for her as soon as possible. Of course. Jim was off-island somewhere just waiting for the storm to be over. He had said he wouldn't risk a night journey.

And it's no wonder a little bit fell off the boat, with all those waves. Just a little, unimportant piece, and probably not off Jim's boat at all. Miranda walked herself firmly off to breakfast, clutching her large handbag and her water bottle. She didn't want to eat. But she did need some more water. She walked past the shops. The shut shops. But then they never had opened, not even on the first day. Which seemed a world away now – the last day. The library was deserted, and the telly turned off. Miranda unplugged it when she couldn't make it come on again.

The island was full of the noise of the sea and the whispering palms. And someone was opening presents in each crackling clump of bamboo. The Reception desk was unmanned. But then it often was. After all, no holidaymakers were expected in today. Not with the weather. And there were no boats at the jetty. But she would check at the sunset bar. That was their spot, where they always met. If any of their boats had come back, they would have moored at the jetty there. Now she had arrived at the dining hall and now she would have to go in for breakfast.

The long hot day went on. The offices at Reception remained deserted. The lunchtime buffet failed to appear. There had been no breakfast. Even the monsoon clouds had deserted her, and stood off in the sky, waiting for the night. The centre of the island was too thick with thorns to risk the path, but Miranda knew she would find the staff quarters quiet and still. As for Aladdin's palace … she couldn't imagine what she might find, what she might see if she could look through those closely barred gates.

Not Todd. She didn't think she would see Todd again.

The shower in her villa gradually stopped. Not even a trickle of hot dusty water came through by the time the midday sun began to journey down the sky. Miranda realized she had never even got dressed. She had been wondering around in her jim-jams all day. She felt so sticky and horrible. Why didn't she just plunge into the warm waters of the lagoon and refresh herself? After all, Gordo's boat would be in soon. She couldn't meet him like this.

That was it. She would take her stuff to the sunset bar, have a little swim and then wait for the boat to pull up. Then she and Gordo could leave together, as quickly as they liked. So she would vacate her chalet and move to the bar. Just to have a little swim. This was not in any way a retreat.

And pull yourself together Miranda, she told herself sharply. It isn't

Gordo's boat you are waiting for. If Gordo and the German divers ever made it to the mainland they will long since have packed up and gone home. It's the boat to take us all home. Me home. Probably everyone would be with them. They would have been scooped up. And then they would all just quietly leave Small Island. Isn't that what was wanted after all?

Alarmed to have put that thought into concrete words, Miranda quickly turned her thoughts to her uber-self and wondered if she would put in an appearance.

But there was no sign of her. The woman was about as much use as a chocolate teapot, thought Miranda, with a certain satisfaction.

The urgency she felt to get away from the villa, right to the edge of the island, and as far away as possible from the empty offices and dining rooms was growing stronger. She looked round their chalet, wondering what she should take with her. Just as if she wouldn't be coming back here again. A ridiculous thought, Miranda, she told herself firmly. After all, if by any chance, they didn't all make it back here till tomorrow morning, then that was where she would be sleeping. But, just for the moment, she wanted to go and sit at the sunset bar. After all, sunset was coming on. It was a reasonable choice surely.

'Shall I irritate you less if I'm perched on the edge of you? You just couldn't bear us, anymore. That's the truth of it, isn't it?'

Miranda was shocked to hear herself saying those words out loud. But they were the simple truth. Yes, Small Island, if this were an Agatha Christie novel, then this would be the moment when the detective would be gathering their island together with a crowd of other islands: Last Year's Island; Somewhat Bigger and a Lot Less Remote Island; Italian Island; and the mythological Island of the Stewardesses that all the diving guys hoped to find.

Yes. He would be gathering them all together. He might even have retrieved Al Nino from the depths of her subconscious. And, after a lot of iffing and butting and misdirection, he would point to you Small Island. Because you did it. You are doing it.

But it wasn't really your fault, was it? You were too young and tender for all our demands. The older islands waited patiently for their rescue to arrive. But you wouldn't. We were too painful for your baby skin. You were allergic to us. And so you got rid of us. One by one. And that is why they tabooed you, why they tried to live so lightly on you.

Miranda found she was cramming things into her large handbag. Socks, her silk shawl. Sun cream. Her mints. She found herself regretting her passport, locked away in the deserted room behind Reception. Her mind shied away from thinking whether or not she could go there again. She picked up her water bottle. About an inch left. Well, that decided it. She would have to go to the bar and wait for the boat. She would have to have more water. It wasn't a question of making a decision. The decision was made. Miranda knew that once she had left her villa she wouldn't be going back to it. She had noticed, sideways, out of the corner of her eye, what had happened to the other villas. No visitors would ever stay in them again. She only made it to the bar by walking along the small edge of beach.

Now it was quiet. Like the first evening of the world. A hush had come over everything. The waves were folding themselves into the beach on tiptoes so as not to wake the little island. It had exhausted itself, tired itself out, and now it slept its boneless baby sleep. Come now. Jim. Mal. Jassie. Anyone. Sail your ship in quietly, tenderly, and get me, whispered Miranda. Before Small Island wakes up and finds I am still here.

She sat at the sunset bar, waiting for her ship to come in. There was no-one behind the bar. No Mo. The Dive Shop was empty. No Wolfie, no Samir, no Jassie. But then Samir would be locked in the thorny heart of the island, with Inga, his sleeping princess. Or they were long gone.

And Ali. The omelette chef. Where was he?

Diane and Alison were drifting out there somewhere. Giggling and

135

snorkelling. Patrick and Patricia still sailed on, towards their hospital bed on a mainland that had certainly existed – was it only a week ago – when their plane touched down on it. And Wolfie and Jassie were perhaps having a belated honeymoon. Where did people honeymoon if they usually lived and worked on honeymoon island? An airport hotel? The central reservation of the M1?

And Jim?

But this was just a dream anyway. It had to be. It was like a dream she once had of another tropical island. A dream of being left alone – completely alone in the darkness. On a beach, with the sea coming, from somewhere. When she woke from that dream, she was alone. In darkness. No Jim. It wasn't till she had put her hand down and felt carpet that she had known where she was. She had been back at home, in the attic bedroom of her childhood. It was after her mother had died. Jim had had to go back to the company after the funeral, and she had stayed on in the empty house for a while. It was the first time in all her life she had ever been completely without parents. It seemed that, one minute they had been young, hopeful, in love. Full of laughter and plans for a perfect future. And then Miranda was standing staring at the memorial stone that was all that was left of them.

If an able-bodied man dies can he live again?

Oh, that you would set a time limit for me and remember me.

Their holly tree still loomed at the bedroom window, sleek and glossy in the wintery sunset.

It wasn't yet dark. But it soon would be. The sun was beginning to set gloriously behind the reef, slipping down beyond the channel to the open ocean. And there was sand underneath Miranda's fingers. Not carpet. Silky white sand. Oh! And something sharp. She wiped the blood off her hand and looked down. Thorns. They had got into the sunset bar now! There were no gardeners to interfere. Small Island could do what it wanted.

Could Gordo and the German divers still be out there somewhere waiting for the waves to die down and the path to Small Island become clear again? But they wouldn't come, would they? No-one would come here again. Perhaps she was sitting right in the middle of her novel after all, as if you waited for Gordo in a fictional world, he was sure not to turn up. Face it, Miranda. Just face it. Small Island won't let anyone else come here. Ever. It had had enough of them. It had had enough of their showers like Niagara, and their cow-pie steaks – their endless, wasteful buffets.

It was young. It was impatient. It felt things so much.

There was no cavalry coming to rescue Miranda. There was no boat. There was no helicopter. She stood up. And it wasn't easy. Because the thorns were encroaching everywhere. She had no shell to protect her, like Inga, sleeping safely in her bubble. She had no Island Man to love her. The thought came, again deeply disturbing, that if the Island Man loved Inga, then Small Island could love her, too. Maybe it would keep them there, safely sleeping, until …

But if Small Island could love, then it could also hate. And it was getting angrier and angrier. When it woke up and found that there was still one irritant left, one allergen, what would it do? Miranda thought she knew. Those bushes were growing so fast she could almost see them grow. She would keep her eye on them. She would watch them as closely as she could. They wouldn't dare grow while she was watching them.

Do you have eyes in the back of your head, Miranda? whispered the sandy beach and the small island palms. The hermit crabs scuttled around, sensibly shopping for shell.

Where is your shell Miranda? Small Island sang softly in her ear. How was she to stay here without one?

There was another shell on the island though. It belonged to Aladdin and his entourage. They had their high walled palace-villa, with its gates so finely woven that nothing unwanted could slip through. Suppose she went and hammered at those gates? What would she find inside?

Nothing and no-one? Just the faintest hint of an incense fragrance, the distant tinkle of bells that once danced on slender, golden ankles? Or would she find Todd, in stewardess-heaven, dancing away safe till doomsday? And would that be better or worse than the thorny fate Small Island had in store for her?

She knew though that whatever she found in the palace of Aladdin, she wouldn't find Todd. Or any air hostesses. But no-one could go into the interior of the island anymore. Not even to their chalet. She would have to sit here until the boat came.

She truly had no home now.

And surely a boat would come. Jim would come back for her. The sea swelled and roared over the house reef, as if the storm still rampaged out there. Perhaps there never was a storm. Or perhaps it stopped ages ago, but Small Island had cut all the cables and kept churning up the water with its long fingers of reef. That brought the thought of fingers of green wavering in the water just after she heard giggling and laughter. And screams. No! Think of something else, Miranda.

Inga. She suddenly thought of Inga, so pale, being helped out of the water, and disappearing into her thorny castle. Safe and sound. Until her prince came to wake her. Did you do that, Small Island? Was that your finger of reef out there? Did you just pull her down a little bit? Just enough? And did you change your current for a moment when Diane and Alison were snorkelling? Did you change the friendly current that pulls us safely round the island, and repel them? Or did you change the currents and bring something to them? Something not so small? Miranda shuddered, remembering the green fingers snaking up from the ocean depths.

Small Island. Please don't have done that. No, you swept them off to the fabled Italian Island, where there are three gorgeous dark eyed guys for every girl. And you have sent Mal after them. For a happy reunion. A kiss and make up.

Miranda tried not to see as the empty windsurfer came careering along once again. Caught in the current beyond the reef top, it whirled madly round the island, veering crazily. Sometimes on its right side, sometimes on its left. Sometimes standing threateningly above the waves. Anyone who sat there and waited for it to come round and round and round in its mad perpetual motion would go stark staring crazy themselves. Miranda simply refused to be aware of it.

Small Island had come close to manslaughter though when it shook its palm trees petulantly and hurled a coconut at poor Patrick's head. That certainly got rid of him and Trish. It was getting angrier. And Todd? Did it lure him somehow, or was he smart enough to find his own shell? What was inside those palatial gates?

And Jim …? Once you leave the island, it won't let you back. Not now.

Had Small Island simply spat them out? As if they were poison? Or was she going mad? She suddenly thought of Chessman, rustling through the bushes with her on the first sleepless night after they arrived. She remembered the splashing and the rustlings, the feeling of Something Small following along after her. That was Small Island too, wasn't it? It had rustled its bushes beside her, and splashed its waters. Very cleverly. But she didn't really notice. She was too tired to take the warning. The island had probably been rustling away at poor Trish too, as she sobbed her heart out under the bushes. But she had other things on her mind. And she didn't listen either. We didn't know it was taboo. The glossy brochure had never told us that.

DEPARTURE

What would Carmen do? But the wretched woman provided as little help as usual. She was nowhere to be found. Probably she had already left. Apparently taking Al Nino with her. Yes. That was it. After giving Small Island's bottom a sound kicking, she would have made for the open seas, with her entourage of hairdressers in tow. She would be clad in a white bikini, her teeth gleaming horribly out of her full body tan, scaring off any sharks foolish enough to lurk about in her vicinity. Yes – she would have speed-boated out of here, cresting the waves, and kicking posterior as she went.

Still she could hardly blame the woman. Getting away from Small Island had to be the right option.

And now Miranda thought that when the baby island woke up and found her still there it would either sting her to death or push her into the sea. And she would much rather jump before she was pushed.

She looked around wildly. There were no boats left. A few windsurfers. But, while Carmen Miranda might be able to speed off like that, Miranda herself would die of old age before she even managed to stand upright on one of the things. And she didn't think that Small Island was going to let her die of old age.

She stood up. Which proved to be a mistake.

When she looked down again, to find her dark glasses, the thorns had almost covered the wooden step. She only just managed to snatch her glasses from them. So she no longer had even a wooden step to call home. Whatever she was going to do, she would have to do it quickly. She thought of Emily. Do it for Emily.

Miranda thought of all the careful plans she and Jim had made, the little cottage they had bought in the Dales, and never yet lived in. Big enough for their Emily and grandchildren, when they arrived. None of it seemed to matter enough to move Miranda. Not now. Because what was the point of any of it without Jim to share it?

She stared vacantly into the mangroves. They had grown so much since the start of the week! That's the tropics – lush to the nth degree. At least they weren't thorny though. The bamboo seemed taller and clumpier too. It rustled and crackled round the island edge.

Chessman!

How could he get by without at least one of them? Who would provide a loving home for such a cantankerous, battered old creature as Chess was, if they weren't around to do it? At least one of them had to get through. Do something, Miranda!

The thought of Chessman seemed to have conjured up the Bathroom Cockroach, who was watching her from a mangrove leaf. Miranda found herself oddly relieved to know that it would be alright. It would probably even enjoy the thorny cover.

Cockroaches might well be an import to the islands, but they didn't demand waterfalls of fresh water on constant supply, HP sauce plantations or eggs without yolks.

She had to face it now. She couldn't put it off for another second. It would be light for another half an hour at the most. And if she didn't get off Small Island immediately, then she would actually have to spend the night on the beach. There wouldn't be anywhere else. She would have to spend the night with the monsoon waves approaching from one side, the thorns from the other. And Small Island singing softly to her.

On her own. In pitch darkness. A dying duck in a thunderstorm.

But the moon! There would be a moon, wouldn't there? Or had that deserted her too? Miranda tried to remember its phases. Small Island could not put out the moon and stars. Certainly not. But – Miranda looked at the sky – could it draw clouds to itself? It might want darkness for the deed it was now going to do.

So there was no alternative, no choice to face. She had to get herself off the island, she had to get through that channel to the open sea. In the next few minutes, before the glorious sunset ended. At least she knew to head away from that long finger of island reef that sucked Inga down and into her thorny shell.

But how? How could she escape? Come on Carmen! Where was she now, now that Miranda needed her? Because she would welcome a glamorous and photogenic way of getting off this island. With a few bottom kicks thrown in. She would be happy to find any way off this island. Anything at all. Miranda looked round as the fires of sunset flared at the edge of the world. This was the last blaze of light before the darkness. The clouds were waiting. And the blackness of darkness was coming.

Suddenly galvanized, perhaps ignited by a little of the explosive energy of the sun, Miranda found herself jumping over thorny outgrowths, going back into the bar. While she still could. Water. She would have to have water. There was no point thinking about escape without it. So there wouldn't be any. There just wouldn't. But her worry list was crammed to overflowing, and there wasn't the room anymore for that particular concern. And so she found three large bottles in the bar fridge. All cold. Some things still worked then. That meant Inga would be safe. Her shell would go on functioning. Once again, she felt oddly sure that Inga's love for the island man would protect her. Small Island had no problem with those who lived lightly on it or who loved those who did.

And as for Todd? Were the Aladdin's still dancing on? She looked back into the island interior for a moment. Was there a glow coming from the very centre? A faint sound of music and jingling bells? Was Todd happily partying away with a glamour of blonde air hostesses?

It doesn't matter anyway, Miranda told herself. She couldn't get to him now, and he couldn't get to her. And he was probably more than happy with that.

There were some frozen milks in the humming fridge. Banana flavour. For the Banana Manana cocktails of course! And she had thought it was fresh banana she was drinking. She piled them all up. She wondered why though, as she was hardly going to be able to swim with that lot.

Because, if necessary, she knew she was going to swim out of there. If necessary! There were no boats left. She couldn't stay through the night, and …

The sun still flared away on the horizon, although the palms were now burnt black. It even threw a red path for her that would lead her right through the channel to the open water beyond. If she could get through there and swim straight away from the reef, she might just do it. She might just get away while the little island slept.

But, what then? She would be out in the vast ocean, night coming, holding desperately on to a bottle of water as a flotation device. Her feet would be in that hungry ocean, unprotected.

Miranda shuddered. Which was worse. A night on her own on Small Island. Or the open ocean?

There was a terrific WHIRR right next to her ear. Miranda jumped, dropping a bottle as the Bathroom Cockroach flew right past her face. It landed just beyond her, on the beach, on that Reliant Robin of beach gear, the pedalo. She snatched the bottle back from the thorns, just in time.

The pedalo. The Bathroom Cockroach whirred back again, past her other ear. And back to the pedalo. It was a battered old plastic one. In a dull shade of blue. Sturdy and slow and sensible. The thorns hadn't bothered with it yet. Miranda found herself standing by it. Then suddenly she (or was it Carmen?) was jumping over encroaching thorns, back and forwards to the bar, loading up the milk and water in the pedalo's chunky, built-in plastic box. Not that she was going out there in the deep ocean, on a pedalo! Most certainly not. And she knew for sure Carmen wasn't. Carmen would rather die. What on earth am I doing, Miranda asked herself, as she crammed as much liquid into the box on the comical blue plastic float as it would hold. Amazingly she was in her jim jams still. So her arms and legs were covered. Which meant she would have only her feet and hands to worry about when the morning sun came up.

Suddenly Miranda was thinking of the morning after the black night that was coming. Maybe this night wouldn't stop the world after all.

There was even a faded canvas awning on the unglamorous piece of plastic. And she still had her bag. The thorns had not yet snatched it from her. So she had her sun cream, her silk shawl, her dark glasses. Didn't she even throw a spare pair of knickers and some socks in during that frantic leaving of the chalet?

Jim's voice spoke in her head, 'Everything but the kitchen sink. Oh, I see you've got that too!'

And was she actually going to pedalo out of here?

If so, she was going to have to do it now. Now. Because the rising tide was already lapping around the plastic pedals. And the thorns seemed to be coming in faster waves. She untied the frayed rope and pushed a bit. What a comedown, Miranda thought, as she clambered into the plastic seat. Her bag was firmly wedged behind her feet, the strap looped securely around her ankles.

What a shabby exit, after Carmen Miranda's glorious technicolour ride. Because here Miranda was, pedaloing off into the sunset. Laden down with banana milk and a spare pair of knickers.

What had she done? What sort of a novel was this going to be? She seemed to be starring in a story that Hollywood couldn't film, even if it wanted to. They'd never get Tom Cruise to play that cockroach. No matter how much they offered him.

Could she fit that worry about casting on to her list? Yes, she thought she profitably could. Because then she definitely wouldn't be able to fit in any worries about sinking pedalos, the deep ocean and all that lay beneath. And the teeth. The many white teeth of the white-frilled ocean.

But Carmen Miranda's teeth! Surely she could worry about them. Because should the woman ever come across something whose bottom she was unable to kick, then she herself might wither and die, but those terrible white teeth would surely go on forever. Scuttling across the sea bottom, pulling down unwary divers, ripping holes in the bottom of atomic submarines and cruise liners.

Yes, that was a good worry. She would worry about that. That would keep the list nice and full. So thank goodness, hers really wasn't a bodice worth ripping. Miranda laughed weakly, and tears ran down her face. She'd be rescued long before she could get round to worrying about Jim, and all the others, and being out in the deep ocean on a pedalo. So, as far as she was concerned, plastic was unsinkable.

Miranda pedalled hard. And the pedalo rolled slowly into the lagoon, towards the channel where the setting sun was lingering, waiting for her. The Bathroom Cockroach took off, whirring a Bon Voyage, before returning to the thorny interior of his enchanted island. She hoped he wasn't really a Fairy Prince, under a spell, because she didn't think Inga would kiss a cockroach under any circumstances. Should she have kissed him gratefully?

But, no, the Bathroom Cockroach would have wanted Inga's kiss. Not middle-aged Miranda's. Her kisses wouldn't work. She could probably kiss him till she was blue in the face and he would still be as cockroachy as ever. Now there was another worry she could fit on to her list. And just suppose she had kissed him, and he had stayed the same, but she, Miranda, had turned into a beautiful lady cockroach. A Cockroach Princess. How embarrassing that would have been. Yes, that was a good worry. She would keep that one.

And, anyway, she thought, she didn't need to kiss any more

cockroaches. She had found her Prince. Many years ago. He was lost to her just now, but she was going to find him again. And then they would resume living happily ever after. She pedalled on towards the sinking sun.

Goodbye Small Island. Miranda waved back to it. You win. You got rid of all of us. Even Carmen Miranda and Al, her consort. I suppose I can thank you for that at least. And now I'm going. You won't see me again.

Wide awake now; blind in its fury, tempestuous in its tantrum, Small Island surged its waves, as if trying to pull her back to the thorny shore, and impale her there. But Miranda pedalled steadily along into the sunset. For she was pulled by a far stronger magnet than the tides of Small Island. She knew that Jim was out there somewhere, waiting for her. She just had to get to him.

If I close my eyes, thought Miranda, I can almost see him. He's floating along on a raft made of driftwood and Boy Scout knots. It's a raft built for two. And he's splashing gently through the warm turquoise ocean, passing the time till I pedalo alongside, reading *The Bumper Book of Shark Attacks on Shipwreck Survivors* with mild detached interest.

The End

If you have enjoyed this story, please consider leaving a review for Sue to let her know what you thought of her work.

Also by Sue Knight

Till They Dropped – now available as an audio short.

'A perfect gem of a story that comes satisfyingly full circle yet ends on a shiver.'

You can find out more about Sue on her author page on the Fantastic Books Store. While you're there, why not browse our delightful tales and wonderfully woven prose?

www.fantasticbooksstore.com